JULIAN BARNES

Julian Barnes is the author of twelve novels, including *The Sense of an Ending*, which won the 2011 Man Booker Prize for Fiction. He has also written three books of short stories, *Cross Channel*, *The Lemon Table* and *Pulse*; four collections of essays; and two books of non-fiction, *Nothing to Be Frightened Of* and the *Sunday Times* number one bestseller *Levels of Life*. He lives in London.

D0048763

ALSO BY JULIAN BARNES

Fiction

Metroland
Before She Met Me
Flaubert's Parrot
Staring at the Sun
A History of the World in 10½ Chapters
Talking it Over
The Porcupine
Cross Channel
England, England
Love, etc
The Lemon Table
Arthur & George
Pulse
The Sense of an Ending

Non-fiction

Letters from London 1990–1995
Something to Declare
The Pedant in the Kitchen
Nothing to Be Frightened Of
Through the Window
Levels of Life
Keeping an Eye Open

Translation

In the Land of Pain
by Alphonse Daudet

JULIAN BARNES

The Noise of Time

VINTAGE

7 9 10 8 6

Vintage
20 Vauxhall Bridge Road,
London SW1V 2SA

Vintage is part of the Penguin Random House
group of companies whose addresses can be found at
global.penguinrandomhouse.com

Penguin
Random House
UK

Page 150, from 'A Career' in the collection *Early Poems* by Yevgeny
Yevtushenko, translated by George Reavey. Published in 1989 in
Great Britain and the United States by Marion Boyars Publishers,
London.

First published in paperback by Vintage in 2017
First published in hardback by Jonathan Cape in 2016

penguin.co.uk/vintage

A CIP catalogue record for this book is
available from the British Library

ISBN 9781784703332

Printed and bound by Clays Ltd, St Ives plc

Penguin Random House is committed to a sustainable future
for our business, our readers and our planet. This book is made
from Forest Stewardship Council® certified paper.

for Pat

One to hear
One to remember
And one to drink.

traditional

It happened in the middle of wartime, on a station platform as flat and dusty as the endless plain surrounding it. The idling train was two days out from Moscow, heading east; another two or three to go, depending on coal and troop movements. It was shortly after dawn, but the man — in reality, only half a man — was already propelling himself towards the soft carriages on a low trolley with wooden wheels. There was no way of steering it except to wrench at the contraption's front edge; and to stop himself from overbalancing, a rope that passed underneath the trolley was looped through the top of his trousers. The man's hands were bound with blackened strips of cloth, and his skin hardened from begging on streets and stations.

His father had been a survivor of the previous war. Blessed by the village priest, he had set off to fight for his homeland and the Tsar. By the time he returned, priest and Tsar were gone, and his homeland was not the same. His wife had screamed when she saw what war had done to her husband. Now there was another war, and the same invader was back, except that the names had changed: names on both sides. But nothing else had changed: young men were still blown to bits by guns, then roughly sliced by surgeons. His own legs had been removed in a field hospital among broken trees. It was all in a great cause, as it had been the time before. He did not give a fuck. Let others argue about that; his only concern was to get to the end of each day. He had become a technique for survival. Below a certain point, that was what all men became: techniques for survival.

A few passengers had descended to take the dusty air; others had their faces at the carriage windows. As the beggar approached, he would start roaring out a filthy barrack-room song. Some passengers might toss him a kopeck or two for the entertainment; others pay him to move on. Some deliberately threw coins to land on their edge and roll away, and would laugh as he chased after them, his fists working against the concrete platform. This might make others, out of pity or shame, hand over money more directly. He saw only fingers, coins and coat-sleeves, and was impervious to insult. This was the one who drank.

The two men travelling in soft class were at a window, trying to guess where they were and how long they might be stopping for: minutes, hours, perhaps the whole day. No information was given out, and they knew not to ask. Enquiring about the movement of trains – even if you were a passenger on one – could mark you as a saboteur. The men were in their thirties, well old enough to have learnt such lessons. The one who heard was a thin, nervous fellow with spectacles; around his neck and wrists he wore amulets of garlic. His travelling companion's name is lost to history, even though he was the one who remembered.

The trolley with the half-man aboard now rattled towards them. Cheerful lines about some village rape were bellowed up at them. The singer paused and made the eating sign. In reply, the man with spectacles held up a bottle of vodka. It was a needless gesture of politeness. When had a beggar ever turned down vodka? A minute later, the two passengers joined him on the platform.

And so there were three of them, the traditional vodka-drinking number. The one with spectacles still had the bottle, his companion three glasses. These were filled approximately, and the two travellers bent from the waist and uttered the routine toast to health. As they clinked glasses, the nervous fellow put his head on one side – the early-morning sun flashing briefly on his spectacles – and murmured a remark; his friend laughed. Then they threw the vodka down in one go. The beggar held up his glass for more. They gave him another shot, took the glass from him, and climbed back on the train. Thankful *for the burst of alcohol coursing through his truncated body, the beggar wheeled himself towards the next group of passengers. By the time the two men were in their seats again, the one who heard had almost forgotten what he had said. But the one who remembered was only at the start of his remembering.*

1: On the Landing

All he knew was that this was the worst time.

He had been standing by the lift for three hours. He was on his fifth cigarette, and his mind was skittering.

Faces, names, memories. Cut peat weighing down his hand. Swedish water birds flickering above his head. Fields of sunflowers. The smell of carnation oil. The warm, sweet smell of Nita coming off the tennis court. Sweat oozing from a widow's peak. Faces, names.

The faces and names of the dead, too.

He could have brought a chair from the apartment. But his nerves would in any case have kept him upright. And it would look decidedly eccentric, sitting down to wait for the lift.

His situation had come out of the blue, and yet it was perfectly logical. Like the rest of life. Like sexual desire, for instance. That came out of the blue, and yet it was perfectly logical.

★

He tried to keep his mind on Nita, but his mind disobeyed. It was like a bluebottle, noisy and promiscuous. It landed on Tanya, of course. But then off it buzzed to that girl, that Rozaliya. Did he blush to remember her, or was he secretly proud of that perverse incident?

The Marshal's patronage – that had also come out of the blue, and yet it was perfectly logical. Could the same be said of the Marshal's fate?

Jurgensen's affable, bearded face; and with it, the memory of his mother's fierce, angry fingers around his wrist. And his father, his sweet-natured, lovable, impractical father, standing by the piano and singing 'The Chrysanthemums in the Garden Have Long Since Faded'.

The cacophony of sounds in his head. His father's voice, the waltzes and polkas he had played while courting Nita, four blasts of a factory siren in F sharp, dogs outbarking an insecure bassoonist, a riot of percussion and brass beneath a steel-lined government box.

These noises were interrupted by one from the real world: the sudden whirr and growl of the lift's machinery. Now it was his foot that skittered, knocking over the little case that rested against his calf. He waited, suddenly empty of memory, filled only with fear. Then the lift stopped at a lower floor, and his faculties re-engaged. He picked up his case and felt the contents softly shift.

Which made his mind jump to the story of Prokofiev's pyjamas.

No, not like a bluebottle. More like one of those mosquitoes in Anapa. Landing anywhere, drawing blood.

He had thought, standing here, that he would be in charge of his mind. But at night, alone, it seemed that his mind was in charge of him. Well, there is no escaping one's destiny, as the poet assured us. And no escaping one's mind.

He remembered the pain that night before they took his appendix out. Throwing up twenty-two times, swearing all the swear-words he knew at a nurse, then begging a friend to fetch the militiaman to shoot him and end the pain. Get him to come in and shoot me to end the pain, he had pleaded. But the friend had refused to help.

He didn't need a friend and a militiaman now. There were enough volunteers already.

It had all begun, very precisely, he told his mind, on the morning of the 28th of January 1936, at Arkhangelsk railway station. No, his mind responded, nothing begins just like that, on a certain date at a certain place. It all began in many places, and at many times, some even before you were born, in foreign countries, and in the minds of others.

★

And afterwards, whatever might happen next, it would all continue in the same way, in other places, and in the minds of others.

He thought of cigarettes: packs of Kazbek, Belomor, Herzegovina Flor. Of a man crumbling the tobacco from half a dozen papirosy into his pipe, leaving on the desk a debris of cardboard tubes and paper.

Could it, even at this late stage, be mended, put back, reversed? He knew the answer: what the doctor said about the restoration of The Nose. 'Of course it can be put back, but I assure you, you will be the worse for it.'

He thought about Zakrevsky, and the Big House, and who might have replaced Zakrevsky there. Someone would have done. There was never a shortage of Zakrevskys, not in this world, constituted as it was. Perhaps when Paradise was achieved, in almost exactly 200,000,000,000 years' time, the Zakrevskys would no longer need to exist.

At moments his mind refused to believe what was happening. It can't be, because it couldn't ever be, as the Major said when he saw the giraffe. But it could be, and it was.

Destiny. It was just a grand term for something you could do nothing about. When life said to you, 'And so,' you nodded, and called it destiny. And so, it had been his destiny to be called Dmitri Dmitrievich. There was nothing to be done about that. Naturally, he didn't remember his own christening, but had no reason to doubt the truth of the story. The family had all assembled in his father's study around a portable font. The priest arrived, and asked his parents what name they intended for the newborn. Yaroslav, they had replied. Yaroslav? The priest was not happy with this. He said that it was a most unusual name. He said that children with unusual names were teased and mocked at school: no, no, they couldn't call the boy Yaroslav. His father and mother were perplexed by such forthright opposition, but didn't wish to give offence. What name do you suggest then? they asked. Call him something ordinary, said the priest: Dmitri, for instance. His father pointed out that he himself was already called Dmitri, and that Yaroslav Dmitrievich sounded much better than Dmitri Dmitrievich. But the priest did not agree. And so he became Dmitri Dmitrievich.

What did a name matter? He had been born in St Petersburg, started growing up in Petrograd, finished growing up in Leningrad. Or St Leninsburg, as he sometimes liked to call it. What did a name matter?

He was thirty-one. His wife Nita lay a few yards away with their daughter, Galina, at her side. Galya was a year old. Recently, his life had appeared to acquire stability. He had never found that side of things straightforward. He felt powerful emotions but had never become skilled at expressing them. Even at a football match he rarely yelled and lost control of himself like everyone else; he was content with the quiet annotation of a player's skill, or lack of it. Some thought this the typical buttoned-up formality of a Leningrader; but on top of that – or underneath it – he knew he was a shy and anxious person. And with women, when he lost his shyness, he veered between absurd enthusiasm and lurching despair. It was as if he was always on the wrong metronome setting.

Still, even so, his life had finally acquired some regularity, and with it the correct beat. Except that now it had all become unstable again. Unstable: that was more than a euphemism.

The overnight case resting against his calf reminded him of the time he had tried to run away from home. How old had he been? Seven or eight, perhaps. And did he have a little suitcase with him? Probably not – his mother's exasperation would have been too immediate. It was one summer at Irinovka, where his father worked as general manager. Jurgensen was the estate's handyman. Who made things and mended things, who solved problems in the way a child could understand. Who never instructed him to do anything, just let him watch as a piece of wood turned into a dagger or a whistle. Who handed him a piece of fresh-cut peat and allowed him to sniff it.

He had become very attached to Jurgensen. So when things displeased him, as they frequently did, he would say, 'Very well then, I'll go and live with Jurgensen.' One morning, still in bed, he had made this threat, or promise, for the first time that day. But once was already enough for his mother. Get dressed and I'll take you there, she had replied. He took up her challenge – no, there had been no time to pack – Sofya Vasilyevna had taken him firmly by the wrist, and they had started walking across the field to where Jurgensen lived. At

· 12 ·

first he had been bold in his threat, swaggering along beside his mother. But gradually his heels dragged, and his wrist, then hand, began to slip from his mother's grasp. He thought at the time it was he who was pulling away, but now acknowledged that his mother had been letting him go, finger by finger, until he was free. Not free to live with Jurgensen, but free to turn tail, burst into tears, and run home.

Hands, slipping hands, grabbing hands. As a child, he had feared the dead – feared that they would rise from their graves and seize hold of him, dragging him back into the cold, black earth, his mouth and eyes filling with soil. This fear had slowly disappeared, because the hands of the living had turned out to be more frightening. The prostitutes of Petrograd had been no respecters of his youth and innocence. The harder the times, the grabbier the hands. Stretching out to seize your cock, your bread, your friends, your family, your livelihood, your existence. As well as prostitutes, he had been afraid of janitors. Also of policemen, whatever names they chose to call themselves by.

But then there was the opposite fear: of slipping from hands that kept you safe.

Marshal Tukhachevsky had kept him safe. For many years. Until the day he had watched the sweat march down from the Marshal's hairline. A large white handkerchief had fluttered and dabbed, and he knew he wasn't safe any more.

★

The Marshal was the most sophisticated man he had ever encountered. He was Russia's most famous military strategist: newspapers called him 'The Red Napoleon'. Also a music lover and amateur violin maker; a man of open, questioning mind, who enjoyed discussing novels. In the decade he had known Tukhachevsky, he had often seen him sweeping through Moscow and Leningrad after dark in his Marshal's uniform, half at work, half at play, mixing politics with pleasure; talking and arguing, eating and drinking, keen to show that he had an eye for a ballerina. He liked to explain how the French had once taught him the secret of drinking champagne without ever getting a hangover.

He himself would never be as worldly. He lacked the self-confidence; also, perhaps, the interest. He didn't like complicated food, and had a light head for drink. Back when he was a student, when everything was being rethought and remade, before the Party took full control, he had, like most students, claimed a sophistication beyond what he knew. For instance, the question of sex had to be rethought, now that the old ways were gone for ever; and someone had come up with the 'glass of water' theory. The act of sex, young know-alls maintained, was just like drinking a glass of water: when you were thirsty, you drank, and when you felt desire, you had sex. He had not been against this system, though it did depend on women being as freely desirous as they were desired. Some were, some weren't. But the analogy only took you so far. A glass of water did not engage the heart.

And besides, Tanya had already come into his life by then.

When he used to announce his regular intention of going to live with Jurgensen, his parents probably assumed he was chafing at the restrictions of family – even of childhood itself. Now that he thought about it, he wasn't so sure. There had been something odd – something deeply wrong – about that summer house of theirs on the estate at Irinovka. Like any child, he assumed things were normal until told otherwise. So it was only when he heard the grown-ups discussing it, and laughing, that he realised how everything about the house was out of proportion. The rooms were enormous, but the windows very small. So a room of fifty square metres might have just one tiny window. The grown-ups thought the builders must have muddled their measurements, substituting metres for centimetres, and vice versa. But the effect, once you noticed it, was alarming to a boy. It was like a house prepared for the darkest of dreams. Maybe that was what he'd been running away from.

They always came for you in the middle of the night. And so, rather than be dragged from the apartment in his pyjamas, or forced to dress in front of some contemptuously impassive NKVD man, he would go to bed fully clothed, lying on top of the blankets, a small case already packed on the floor beside him. He barely slept, and lay there imagining the worst things a man could imagine. His restlessness in turn prevented Nita from sleeping. Each would lie there, pretending; also, pretending not to hear and smell the other's terror. One of his persistent waking nightmares was that the NKVD would seize Galya and pack her off – if she was lucky – to a special orphanage for children of enemies of the state. Where she would be given a new name and a new character; where she would be turned into a model Soviet citizen, a little sunflower lifting her face towards the great sun that called itself Stalin. He had therefore proposed that he spend those inevitably sleepless hours out on the landing by the lift. Nita was adamant that she wanted them to spend what might prove their last night together side by side. But this was a rare argument he won.

On his first night by the lift, he had decided not to smoke. There were three packs of Kazbeki in his case, and he would need them when it came to his interrogation. And, if it followed, his detention. He held to this resolve through the first two nights. And then it struck him: what if they confiscated his cigarettes as soon as he reached the Big House? Or what if there was no interrogation, or only the briefest of ones? Perhaps they would merely put a sheet of paper in front of him and order him to sign. What if . . . His mind went no further. But in any of these cases, his cigarettes would have been wasted.

And so he couldn't think of a reason not to smoke.

And so he smoked.

He looked at the Kazbek between his fingers. Malko had once commented in a sympathetic, indeed admiring, way that his hands were small and 'non-pianistic'. Malko had also told him, less admiringly, that he didn't practise enough. It depended what you meant by 'enough'. He practised as much as he needed to. Malko should stick to his score and his baton.

He had been sixteen, at a sanatorium in the Crimea, recovering from tuberculosis. Tanya and he were the same age, and shared exactly the same birth date, with one small difference: he was born on the 25th of September New Style, she on the 25th of September Old Style. Such virtual synchronicity endorsed their relationship; or, to put it another way, they were made for one another. Tatyana Glivenko, with her short-cropped hair, as eager for life as he was. It was first love, in all its apparent simplicity, and in all its destiny. His sister Marusya, who was chaperoning him, had blabbed to their mother. By return of post Sofya Vasilyevna warned her son against this unknown girl, against this relationship – indeed, any relationship. In reply, with all the pomposity of a sixteen-year-old, he had explained to his mother the principles of Free Love. How all must be free to love as they wished; how carnal love lasted but a short time; how the sexes were entirely equal; how marriage ought to be abolished as an institution, but that if it continued in practice, the woman had the full right to an affair if she so desired, and if she then wanted a divorce, the man must accept it and take the blame; but how, in all of this, and despite everything, the children were sacred.

His mother had not replied to his condescending and sanctimonious explanation of life. And in any case, he and Tanya were to part almost as soon as they had met. She returned to Moscow; he and Marusya to Petrograd. But he wrote to her constantly; they visited one another; and he dedicated his first piano trio to her. His mother continued not to approve. And then, three years later, they finally spent those weeks together in the Caucasus. They were each nineteen and unaccompanied; and he had just made three hundred roubles playing concerts in Kharkov. Those weeks in Anapa together . . . how long ago they felt. Well, how long ago they were – more than a third of his life away.

And so, it had all begun, very precisely, on the morning of the 28th of January 1936, in Arkhangelsk. He had been invited to perform his first piano concerto with the local orchestra under Viktor Kubatsky; the two of them had also played his new cello sonata. It had gone well. The next morning he went to the railway station to buy a copy of *Pravda*. He had looked at the front page briefly, then turned to the next two. It was, as he would later put it, the most memorable day of his life. And a date he chose to mark each year until his death.

Except that – as his mind obstinately argued back – nothing ever begins as precisely as that. It began in different places, and in different minds. The true starting point might have been his own fame. Or his opera. Or it might have been Stalin, who, being infallible, was therefore responsible for everything. Or it could have been caused by something as simple as the layout of an orchestra. Indeed, that might finally be the best way of looking at it: a composer first denounced and humiliated, later arrested and shot, all because of the layout of an orchestra.

If it all began elsewhere, and in the minds of others, then perhaps he could blame Shakespeare, for having written *Macbeth*. Or Leskov for Russifying it into *Lady Macbeth of Mtsensk*. No, none of that. It was, self-evidently, his own fault for having written the piece that offended. It was his opera's fault for being such a success – at home and abroad – it had aroused the curiosity of the Kremlin. It was Stalin's fault because he would have inspired and approved the *Pravda* editorial – perhaps even written it himself: there were enough grammatical errors to suggest the pen of one whose mistakes could never be corrected. It was also Stalin's fault for imagining himself a patron and connoisseur of the arts in the first place.

He was known never to miss a performance of *Boris Godunov* at the Bolshoi. He was almost as keen on *Prince Igor* and Rimsky-Korsakov's *Sadko*. Why should Stalin not want to hear this acclaimed new opera, *Lady Macbeth of Mtsensk*?

And so, the composer was instructed to attend a performance of his own work on the 26th of January 1936. Comrade Stalin would be there; also Comrades Molotov, Mikoyan and Zhdanov. They took their places in the government box. Which had the misfortune to be situated immediately above the percussion and the brass. Sections which in *Lady Macbeth of Mtsensk* were not scored to behave in a modest and self-effacing fashion.

He remembered looking across from the director's box, where he was seated, to the government box. Stalin was hidden behind a small curtain, an absent presence to whom the other distinguished comrades would sycophantically turn, knowing that they were themselves observed. Given the occasion, both conductor and orchestra were understandably nervous. In the entr'acte before Katerina's wedding, the woodwind and brass suddenly took it upon themselves to play more loudly than he had scored. And then it was like a virus spreading through each section. If the conductor noticed, he was powerless. Louder and louder the orchestra became; and every time the percussion and brass roared fortissimo beneath them – loud enough to knock out window-panes – Comrades Mikoyan and Zhdanov would shudder theatrically, turn to the figure behind the curtain and make some mocking remark. When the audience looked up to the government box at the start of the fourth act, they saw that it had been vacated.

After the performance, he had collected his briefcase and

gone straight to the Northern Station to catch the train for Arkhangelsk. He remembered thinking that the government box had been specially reinforced with steel plates, to protect its occupants against assassination. But that there was no such cladding to the director's box. He was not yet thirty, and his wife was five months pregnant at the time.

1936: he had always been superstitious about leap years. Like many people, he believed that they brought bad luck.

The lift's machinery sounded once more. When he realized that it had passed the fourth floor, he picked up his case and held it by his side. He waited for the doors to open, for the sight of a uniform, a nod of recognition, and then those outstretched hands reaching towards him, and the clamp of fist on wrist. Which would be quite unnecessary, given his eagerness to accompany them, to get them away from the premises, away from his wife and child.

Then the lift doors opened, and it was a neighbour, with a different nod of recognition, designed to give nothing away – not even surprise at seeing him go out at such a late hour. He inclined his head in reply, walked into the lift, pressed a button at random, rode down a couple of floors, waited for a few minutes, then back up to the fifth floor where he got out and resumed his vigil. This had happened before, and in the same way. Words were never exchanged, because words were dangerous. It was just possible that he looked like a man humiliatingly thrown out by his wife, night after night; or a man who indecisively kept walking out on his wife, night after night, and then returning. But it was probable that he looked exactly what he was: a man, like hundreds of others across the city, waiting, night after night, for arrest.

Years ago, lifetimes away, back in the last century, when his mother had been at the Irkutsk Institute for Noblewomen, she and two other girls had danced the mazurka from *A Life for the Tsar* in front of Nicolas II, then crown prince. Glinka's opera was of course unperformable in the Soviet Union, even if its theme – the morally instructive one of a poor peasant who lays down his life for a great leader – might have appealed to Stalin. 'A Dance for the Tsar': he wondered if Zakrevsky knew about that. In the old days, a child might pay for the sins of its father, or indeed mother. Nowadays, in the most advanced society on earth, the parents might pay for the sins of the child, along with uncles, aunts, cousins, in-laws, colleagues, friends, and even the man who unthinkingly smiled at you as he came out of the lift at three in the morning. The system of retribution had been greatly improved, and was so much more inclusive than it used to be.

His mother had been the strength in her marriage, just as Nina Vasilievna was the strength in theirs. His father, Dmitri Boleslavovich, had been a gentle, unworldly man who worked hard and handed his salary to his wife, keeping back just a small amount of tobacco money. He had a fine tenor voice and played four-handed piano. He sang gypsy romances, songs like 'Ah, It Is Not You I Love So Passionately', and 'The Chrysanthemums in the Garden Have Long Since Faded'. He adored toys and games and detective stories. A new-fangled cigarette lighter or a wire puzzle would keep him amused for hours. He did not come at life directly. He had a special rubber stamp made, so that every item in his library was inscribed with the purple words: 'This book has been stolen from D. B. Shostakovich.'

A psychiatrist researching the creative process had once asked him about Dmitri Boleslavovich. He had replied that his father 'was an entirely normal human being'. This was not a patronising phrase: it was an enviable skill to be a normal human being, and to wake up every morning with a smile on your face. Also, his father had died young – in his late forties. A disaster for the family, and for those who loved him; but not, perhaps, a disaster for Dmitri Boleslavovich himself. Had he lived any longer, he would have watched the Revolution turn sour, paranoid and carnivorous. Not that he was much interested in the Revolution. This had been another of his strengths.

On his death his widow had been left with no income, two daughters, and a musically precocious son of fifteen. Sofya Vasilyevna had taken menial jobs to support them. She worked as a typist in the Chamber of Weights and Measures, and gave piano lessons in exchange for bread. Sometimes he wondered if all his anxieties had not begun with his father's death. But he preferred not to believe this, because it came close to blaming Dmitri Boleslavovich. So perhaps it was truer to say that all his anxieties were redoubled at that moment. How many times had he nodded agreement to those gravely encouraging words: 'You must be the man in the family now.' They had freighted him with an expectation and a sense of duty he was ill equipped to bear. And his health had always been delicate: he was all too familiar with the doctor's palpating hands, the tapping and listening, the probe, the knife, the sanatorium. He kept waiting for this promised manliness to develop in him. But he was, he knew, easily distracted; also, wilful rather than continuingly assertive. Hence his failure to set up house with Jurgensen.

His mother was an inflexible woman, both by temperament and necessity. She had protected him, worked for him, loaded all her hopes onto him. Of course he loved her – how could he not? – but there were . . . difficulties. The strong cannot help confronting; the less strong cannot help evading. His father had always avoided difficulties, had cultivated humour and indirection in the face of both his life and his wife. And so the son, though he knew himself more resolute than Dmitri Boleslavovich, rarely challenged his mother's authority.

But he knew that she used to read his diary. So he would deliberately write into it, for a date a few weeks ahead, 'Suicide'. Or, sometimes, 'Marriage'.

She had her own threats too. Whenever he tried to leave home, Sofya Vasilyevna would say to others, but in his presence, 'My son will first have to step over my corpse.'

They were neither of them sure how much the other meant it.

He had been backstage at the Small Hall of the Conservatoire, feeling chastened and sorry for himself. He was still a student, and the first public performance of his music in Moscow had not gone well: the audience had clearly preferred Shebalin's work. Then a man in military uniform appeared at his side with consoling words: and so his friendship with Marshal Tukhachevsky had begun. The Marshal acted as his patron, organising financial support for him from the military commander of the Leningrad District. He had been helpful and true. Most recently, he had told everyone he knew that

Lady Macbeth of Mtsensk was in his opinion the first classic Soviet opera.

Only once so far had he failed. Tukhachevsky was convinced that a move to Moscow was the best way to speed his protégé's career, and promised to arrange the transfer. Sofya Vasilyevna had naturally been against it: her son was too fragile, too delicate. Who would ensure he drank his milk and ate his porridge if his mother was not seeing to it? Tukhachevsky had the power, the influence, the financial resources; but Sofya Vasilyevna still held the key to his soul. And so he had remained in Leningrad.

Like his sisters, he had first been put in front of a keyboard at the age of nine. And that was when the world became clear to him. Or a part of the world, anyway – enough to sustain him for life. Understanding the piano, and music, had come easily – at least, compared to understanding other things. And he had worked hard because it felt easy to work hard. And so, there was no escaping this destiny either. And as the years passed, it seemed all the more miraculous because it gave him a way of supporting his mother and sisters. He was not a conventional man, and theirs had not been a conventional household, but still. Sometimes, after a successful concert, when he had received applause and money, he felt almost capable of becoming that elusive thing, the man in the family. Though at other times, even after he had left home, married and fathered a child, he could still feel like a lost boy.

Those who did not know him, and who followed music only from a distance, probably imagined that this had been his first setback. That the brilliant nineteen-year-old whose First

Symphony was quickly taken up by Bruno Walter, then by Toscanini and Klemperer, had known nothing but a clear, clean decade of success since that premiere in 1926. And such people, perhaps aware that fame often leads to vanity and self-importance, might open their *Pravda* and agree that composers could easily stray from writing the kind of music people wanted to hear. And further, since all composers were employed by the state, that it was the state's duty, if they offended, to intervene and draw them back into greater harmony with their audience. This sounded entirely reasonable, didn't it?

Except that they had practised sharpening their claws on his soul from the beginning: while he was still at the Conservatoire a group of Leftist fellow students had tried to have him dismissed and his stipend removed. Except that the Russian Association of Proletarian Musicians and similar cultural organisations had campaigned from their inception against what he stood for; or rather, what they thought he stood for. They were determined to break the bourgeois stranglehold on the arts. So workers must be trained to become composers, and all music must be instantly comprehensible and pleasing to the masses. Tchaikovsky was decadent, and the slightest experimentation condemned as 'formalism'.

Except that as early as 1929 he had been officially denounced, told that his music was 'straying from the main road of Soviet art', and sacked from his post at the Choreographic Technical College. Except that in the same year Misha Kvadri, the dedicatee of his First Symphony, became the first of his friends and associates to be arrested and shot.

Except that in 1932, when the Party dissolved the independent organisations and took charge of all cultural matters, this had resulted not in a taming of arrogance, bigotry and ignorance, rather in a systematic concentration of them. And if the plan to take a worker from the coal face and turn him into a composer of symphonies did not exactly come to pass, something of the reverse happened. A composer was expected to increase his output just as a coal miner was, and his music was expected to warm hearts just as a miner's coal warmed bodies. Bureaucrats assessed musical output as they did other categories of output; there were established norms, and deviations from those norms.

At Arkhangelsk railway station, opening *Pravda* with chilled fingers, he had found on page three a headline identifying and condemning deviance: MUDDLE INSTEAD OF MUSIC. He determined at once to return home via Moscow, where he would seek advice. On the train, as the frozen landscape passed, he reread the article for the fifth and sixth times. Initially, he had been shocked as much for his opera as for himself: after such a denunciation, *Lady Macbeth of Mtsensk* could not possibly continue at the Bolshoi. For the last two years, it had been applauded everywhere – from New York to Cleveland, from Sweden to Argentina. In Moscow and Leningrad, it had pleased not just the public and the critics, but also the political commissars. At the time of the 17th Party Congress its performances had been listed as part of the Moscow district's official output, which aimed to compete with the production quotas of the Donbass coal miners.

All this meant nothing now: his opera was to be put down like a yapping dog which had suddenly displeased its master. He tried to analyse the different elements of the attack as clear-headedly as possible. First, his opera's very success, especially abroad, was turned against it. Only a few months before, *Pravda* had patriotically reported the work's American premiere at the Metropolitan Opera. Now the same paper knew that *Lady Macbeth of Mtsensk* had only succeeded outside the Soviet Union because it was 'non-political and confusing', and because it 'tickled the perverted taste of the bourgeois with its fidgety, neurotic music'.

Next, and linked to this, was what he thought of as government-box criticism, an articulation of those smirks and yawns and sycophantic turnings towards the hidden Stalin. So he read how his music 'quacks and grunts and growls'; how its 'nervous, convulsive and spasmodic' nature derived from jazz; how it replaced singing with 'shrieking'. The opera had clearly been scribbled down in order to please the 'effete', who had lost all 'wholesome taste' for music, preferring 'a confused stream of sound'. As for the libretto, it deliberately concentrated on the most sordid parts of Leskov's tale: the result was 'coarse, primitive and vulgar'.

But his sins were political as well. So the anonymous analysis by someone who knew as much about music as a pig knows about oranges was decorated with those familiar, vinegar-soaked labels. Petit-bourgeois, formalist, Meyerholdist, Leftist. The composer had written not an opera but an anti-opera, with music deliberately turned inside out. He had drunk from the same poisoned source which produced 'Leftist distortion in painting, poetry, teaching and science'. In case it needed spelling out – and it always did – Leftism was contrasted with 'real art, real science and real literature'.

'Those that have ears will hear,' he always liked to say. But even the stone deaf couldn't fail to hear what 'Muddle Instead of Music' was saying, and guess its likely consequences. There were three phrases which aimed not just at his theoretical misguidedness but at his very person. 'The composer apparently never considered the problem of what the Soviet audience looks for and expects in music.' That was enough to take away his membership of the Union of Composers. 'The danger of this trend to Soviet music is clear.' That was enough to take away his ability to compose and perform. And finally: 'It is a game of clever ingenuity that may end very badly.' That was enough to take away his life.

But still, he was young, confident in his talent, and highly successful until three days ago. And if he was no politician, either by temperament or aptitude, there were people he could turn to. So in Moscow he first addressed himself to Platon Kerzhentsev, President of the Committee for Cultural Affairs. He began by explaining the plan of response he had worked out on the train. He would write a defence of the opera, an argued rebuttal of the criticism, and submit the article to *Pravda*. For instance . . . But Kerzhentsev, civilised and courteous though he was, would not even hear him out. What they were dealing with here was not a bad review, signed by a critic whose opinion might vary according to the day of the week or the state of his digestion. This was a *Pravda* editorial: not some fleeting judgement which might be appealed against, but a policy statement from the highest level. Holy writ, in other words. The only possible course of action open to Dmitri Dmitrievich was to make a public apology, recant his errors, and explain that while composing his opera he had been led astray by the foolish excesses of youth. Beyond this, he should announce an intention of immersing himself forthwith in the folk music of the Soviet Union, which would help redirect him towards all that was authentic, popular and melodious. According to Kerzhentsev, this was the only way he might achieve an eventual return to favour.

He was not a believer. But he had been baptised, and sometimes, when he passed an open church, he would light a candle for his family. And he knew his Bible well. So he was familiar with the notion of sin; also with its public mechanism. The offence, the full confession of the offence, the priest's judgement on the matter, the act of contrition, the forgiveness. Though there were occasions when the sin was too great and not even a priest could forgive it. Yes, he knew the formulae and the protocols, whatever name the church might go by.

His second call was on Marshal Tukhachevsky. The Red Napoleon was still in his forties, a stern, handsome man with a pronounced widow's peak. He listened to all that had happened, cogently analysed his protégé's position, and came up with a strategic proposal which was simple, bold and generous. He, Marshal Tukhachevsky, would write a personal letter of intercession to Comrade Stalin. Dmitri Dmitrievich's relief was intense. He felt light-headed and light-hearted as the Marshal sat down at his desk and straightened a sheet of paper in front of him. But as soon as the man in uniform gripped his pen and started writing, a change came over him. Sweat began to pour from his hair, from his widow's peak down on to his forehead, and from the back of his head down into his collar. One hand made flurrying darts with a handkerchief, the other halting movements with a pen. Such unsoldierly apprehension was not encouraging.

★

The sweat had poured off them at Anapa. It was hot in the Caucasus, and he had never liked the heat. They had gazed at Low Bay beach but he felt no inclination to cool off by taking a swim. They walked in the shade of the forest above the town, and he was bitten by mosquitoes. Then they were cornered by a pack of dogs and almost eaten alive. None of this mattered. They inspected the resort's lighthouse, but while Tanya craned her head upwards, his concentration was on the sweet fold of skin it made at the base of her neck. They visited the old stone gate which was all that remained of the Ottoman fortress, but he was thinking about her calves, and the way their muscles moved as she walked. There was nothing in his life for those weeks except love, music and mosquito bites. The love in his heart, the music in his head, the bites on his skin. Not even paradise was free of insects. But he could hardly resent them. Their bites were ingeniously made in places inaccessible to him; the lotion was based on an extract of carnation flowers. If a mosquito was the cause of her fingers touching his skin and making him smell of carnations, how could he possibly hold anything against the insect?

They were nineteen and they believed in Free Love: keener tourists of each other's bodies than of the resort's attractions. They had thrown off the fossilised dictates of church, of society, of family, and gone away to live as man and wife without being man and wife. This excited them almost as much as the sexual act itself; or was, perhaps, inextricable from it.

But then came all the time they were not in bed together. Free Love may have solved the primary problem, but had not done away with the others. Of course they loved one another; but being all the time in one another's company – even with his 300 roubles and his young fame – was not straightforward.

When he was composing, he always knew exactly what to do; he made the right decisions about what the music – his music – required. And when conductors or soloists wondered politely if *this* might be better, or *that* might be better, he would always reply, 'I'm sure you're right. But let's leave it for now. I'll make that change next time round.' And they were satisfied, and he was too, since he never had any intention of implementing their suggestions. Because his decisions, and his instinct, had been correct.

But away from music . . . that was so different. He became nervous, things blurred in his mind, and he would sometimes make a decision simply in order to have the matter settled rather than because he knew what he wanted. Perhaps his artistic precocity meant that he had avoided those useful years of ordinary growing up. But whatever the cause, he was bad at the practicalities of life, which included, of course, the practicalities of the heart. And so, at Anapa, alongside the exaltations of love and the heady self-satisfaction of sex, he found himself entering a whole new world, one full of unwanted silences, misunderstood hints and scatter-brained planning.

They had returned again to their separate cities, he to Leningrad, she to Moscow. But they would visit one another. One day, he was finishing a piece and asked her to sit with him: her presence made him feel secure. After a while, his mother came in. Looking straight at Tanya, she had said,

'Go out and leave Mitya to finish his work.'

And he had replied, 'No, I want Tanya to stay here. It helps me.'

This was one of the rare occasions when he had stood up to his mother. Perhaps if he had done so more, his life would have been different. Or perhaps not – who could tell? If the Red Napoleon had been outmanoeuvred by Sofya Vasilyevna, what chance did he ever have?

Their time at Anapa had been an idyll. But an idyll, by definition, only becomes an idyll once it has ended. He had discovered love; but he had also begun to discover that love, far from making him 'what he was', far from spreading deep content all over him like carnation oil, would make him self-conscious and indecisive. He loved Tanya most clearly when he was away from her. When they were together, there were expectations on both sides which he was either unable to identify or couldn't respond to. So, for instance, they had gone away to the Caucasus specifically *not* as man and wife, specifically as free equals. Was the purpose of such an adventure to end up as real man and real wife? That seemed illogical.

No, this was not being honest. One of their incompatibilites was that – whatever the equality of words spoken on either side – he had loved her more than she had loved him. He tried to stir her into jealousy, describing flirtations with other women – even seductions, real or imaginary – but this seemed to make her cross rather than jealous. He had also threatened suicide, more than once. He even announced that he had married a ballet dancer, which might conceivably have been the case. But Tanya had laughed it all off. And then she had got married herself. Which only made him love her the more. He implored her to divorce her husband and marry him; again, he threatened suicide. None of this had any effect.

Early on, she had told him, tenderly, that she had been attracted to him because he was pure and open. But if this didn't make her love him as much as he loved her, then he wished it were otherwise. Not that he felt pure and open. They sounded like words designed to keep him in a box.

He found himself reflecting on questions of honesty. Personal honesty, artistic honesty. How they were connected, if indeed they were. And how much of this virtue anyone had, and how long that store would last. He had told friends that if ever he repudiated *Lady Macbeth of Mtsensk*, they were to conclude that he had run out of honesty.

He thought of himself as someone with strong emotions who was unskilled at conveying them. But that was letting himself off too easily; that was still not being honest. In truth, he was a neurotic. He thought he knew what he wanted, he got what he wanted, he didn't want it any more, it went away from him, he wanted it back again. Of course he was indulged, because he was a mother's boy, and a brother with two sisters; also, an artist, who was expected to have an 'artistic temperament'; also, a success, which allowed him to behave with the sudden arrogance of fame. Malko had already accused him to his face of 'growing vanity'. But his under-lying condition was one of high anxiety. He was a thorough-going neurotic. No, again it was worse than that: he was a hysteric. Where did such a temperament come from? Not from his father; nor from his mother. Well, there was no escaping one's temperament. That too was part of one's destiny.

He knew, in his mind, what his ideal of love was —

But the lift had passed the third floor, and then the fourth, and was now stopping in front of him. He picked up his case, the doors opened, and a man he didn't know came out whistling 'The Song of the Counterplan'. Faced with its composer, he broke off in mid-phrase.

He knew, in his mind, what his ideal of love was. It was fully expressed in that Maupassant short story about the young garrison commander of a fortress town on the Mediterranean coast. Antibes, that was it. Anyway, the officer used to go walking in the woods outside the town, where he kept running into the wife of a local functionary, Monsieur Parisse. Naturally enough, he fell in love with her. The woman repeatedly declined his attentions until the day she let him know that her husband would be away for several nights. An assignation was arranged, but at the last minute the wife received a telegram: her husband's business had concluded early, and he would be home that evening. The garrison commander, mad with passion, feigned a military emergency and ordered the town's gates to be closed until the next morning. The returning husband was driven away at bayonet point and obliged to spend the night in the waiting room of Antibes railway station. All so that the officer could enjoy his few hours of love.

True, he could not imagine himself in charge of a fortress, not even a tumbledown Ottoman gateway in a sleepy Black Sea spa town. But the principle applied. This was how you should love – without fear, without barriers, without thought for the morrow. And then, afterwards, without regret.

★

Fine words. Fine sentiments. Yet such behaviour was beyond him. He could imagine a young Lieutenant Tukhachevsky pulling it off, had he ever been a garrison commander. His own case of mad passion . . . well, it would make a different kind of story. He had been on tour with Gauk – a good enough conductor, but a bourgeois through and through. They were in Odessa. This was a couple of years before he and Nita married. At the time he was still trying to make Tanya jealous. Nita as well, probably. After a good dinner, he had come back to the bar of the London Hotel and picked up two girls. Or perhaps they had picked him up. At any rate, they had joined his table. They were both very pretty, and he was immediately attracted to the one called Rozaliya. They had talked of art and literature while he fondled her buttocks. He drove them home in a horse-drawn carriage and the friend looked away while he touched Rozaliya all over. He was in love, that much was clear to him. The two women had arranged to take a steamer to Batumi the next day, and he went to see them off. But the girls never got beyond the pier, where Rozaliya's friend was arrested for being a professional prostitute.

This had come as a surprise to him. At the same time, he felt such a terrible love for Rozochka. He did things like banging his head against the wall, and tearing at his hair; just like a character in a bad novel. Gauk warned him severely against the two women, saying that they were both prostitutes and terrible bitches. But this only increased his excitement – it was all such fun. So much fun that he'd nearly got married to Rozochka. Except that when they got to the registry office in Odessa he realised he'd left his identity documents back at the hotel. And then, somehow – he couldn't even recall why or how – it had all come to an end with him running away in pouring rain at three o'clock in the morning from a boat which had just docked at Sukhumi. What had all that been about?

But the point was, he didn't regret any of it. No barriers, no thought for the morrow. And how come he had nearly married a professional prostitute? Because of the circumstances, he assumed, and some element of *folie à deux*. Also, because of a spirit of contradictoriness within him. 'Mother, this is Rozaliya, my wife. Surely it doesn't come as a surprise? Didn't you read my diary, where I'd written down "Marriage to a prostitute"? It's good for a woman to have a profession, don't you think?' Also, divorce was easily obtainable, so why not? He had felt such love for her, and a few days later he was nearly marrying her, and a few days after that running away from her in the rain. Meanwhile, old man Gauk sat in the restaurant of the London Hotel, trying to decide whether to have one cutlet or two. And who's to say what would have been for the best? You only found out afterwards, when it was too late.

He was an introverted man who was attracted to extroverted women. Was that part of the trouble?

He lit another cigarette. Between art and love, between oppressors and oppressed, there were always cigarettes. He imagined Zakrevsky's successor, behind his desk, holding out a pack of Belomory. He would decline, and offer one of his own Kazbeki. The interrogator would in return refuse, and each would lay his chosen brand on the desk, the dance concluded. Kazbeki were smoked by artists, and the packet's very design suggested freedom: a galloping horse and rider against the background of Mount Kazbek. Stalin himself was said to have personally approved the artwork; though the Great Leader smoked his own brand, Herzegovina Flor. They were specially made for him, with the terrified precision you could imagine. Not that Stalin did anything as simple as put a Herzegovina Flor between his lips. No, he preferred to break off the cardboard tube and then crumble the tobacco into his pipe. Stalin's desk, those in the know told those not in the know, was a terrible mess of discarded paper and cardboard and ash. He knew this – or rather, he had been told this more than once – because nothing about Stalin was deemed too trivial to pass on.

No one else would smoke a Herzegovina Flor in Stalin's presence – unless offered one, when they might slyly attempt to keep it unsmoked and afterwards flourish it like a holy relic. Those who carried out Stalin's orders tended to smoke Belomory. The NKVD smoked Belomory. Its packet design showed a map of Russia; marked in red was the White Sea Canal, after which the cigarettes were named. This Great Soviet Achievement of the early Thirties had been built with convict labour. Unusually, much propaganda was made of this fact. It was claimed that while constructing the canal the convicts were not just helping the nation advance but also 'reforging themselves'. Well, there had been 100,000 labourers, so it was possible that some of them might have been morally improved; but a quarter of them were said to have died, and those clearly had not been reforged. They were just the chips that had flown while the wood was being chopped. And the NKVD would light up their Belomory and picture in the rising smoke new dreams of wielding the axe.

No doubt he had been smoking at the moment Nita came into his life. Nina Varzar, eldest of the three Varzar sisters, straight off the tennis court, exuding cheerfulness, laughter and sweat. Athletic, confident, popular, with such golden hair that it somehow seemed to turn her eyes golden. A qualified physicist, an excellent photographer who had her own darkroom. Not over-interested in domestic matters, it was true; but then neither was he. In a novel, all his life's anxieties, his mixture of strength and weakness, his potential for hysteria – all would have been swirled away in a vortex of love leading to the blissful calm of marriage. But one of life's many disappointments was that it was never a novel, not by Maupassant or anyone else. Well, perhaps a short satirical tale by Gogol.

And so he and Nina met, and they became lovers, but he was still trying to win Tanya back from her husband, and then Tanya fell pregnant, and then he and Nina fixed a day for their wedding, but at the last minute he couldn't face it so failed to turn up and ran away and hid, but still they persevered and a few months later they married, and then Nina took a lover, and they decided their problems were such that they should separate and divorce, and then he took a lover, and they separated and put in the papers for a divorce, but by the time the divorce came through they realised they had made a mistake and so six weeks after the divorce they remarried, but still they had not resolved their troubles. And in the middle of it all he wrote to his lover Yelena, 'I am very weak-willed and do not know if I will be able to achieve happiness.'

And then Nita fell pregnant, and everything of necessity stabilised. Except that, with Nita into her fourth month, the leap year of 1936 began, and on its twenty-sixth day Stalin decided to go to the opera.

★

The first thing he had done after reading the *Pravda* editorial was to telegraph Glikman. He asked his friend to go to the Central Leningrad Post Office and open a subscription to receive all the relevant press cuttings. Glikman would bring them round to his apartment each day, and they would read them through together. He bought a large scrapbook and pasted 'Muddle Instead of Music' onto the first page. Glikman thought this unduly masochistic, but he had said, 'It has to be there, it has to be there.' Then he pasted in every new article as it appeared. He had never bothered keeping reviews before; but this was different. Now they were not just reviewing his music, but editorialising about his existence.

He noted how critics who had consistently praised *Lady Macbeth of Mtsensk* over the past two years suddenly found no merit at all in it. Some candidly admitted their own previous errors, explaining that the *Pravda* article had made the scales fall from their eyes. How greatly they had been duped by the music and its composer! At last they saw what a danger formalism and cosmopolitanism and Leftism presented to the true nature of Russian music! He also noted which musicians now made public statements against his work, and which friends and acquaintances chose to distance themselves from him. With equal apparent calm he read the letters which came in from ordinary members of the public, most of whom just happened to know his private address. Many of them advised him that his ass's ears should be chopped off, along with his head. And then the phrase from which there was no recovery began to appear in the newspapers, inserted into the most normal sentence. For instance: 'Today there is to be held a concert of works by the enemy of the people Shostakovich.' Such words were never used by accident, or without approval from the highest level.

★

Why, he wondered, had Power now turned its attention to music, and to him? Power had always been more interested in the word than the note: writers, not composers, had been proclaimed the engineers of human souls. Writers were condemned on page one of *Pravda*, composers on page three. Two pages apart. And yet it was not nothing: it could make the difference between death and life.

The engineers of human souls: a chilly, mechanistic phrase. And yet . . . what was the artist's business with, if not the human soul? Unless an artist wanted to be merely decorative, or merely a lapdog of the rich and powerful. He himself had always been anti-aristocratic, in feeling, politics, artistic principle. In that optimistic time – really so very few years ago – when the future of the whole country, if not of humanity itself, was being remade, it had seemed as if all the arts might finally come together in one glorious joint project. Music and literature and theatre and film and architecture and ballet and photography would form a dynamic partnership, not just reflecting society or criticising it or satirising it, but *making* it. Artists, of their own free will, and without any political direction, would help their fellow human souls develop and flourish.

Why not? It was the artist's oldest dream. Or, as he now thought, the artist's oldest fantasy. Because the political bureaucrats had soon arrived to take control of the project, to leach out of it the freedom and imagination and complication and nuance without which the arts grew stultified. 'The engineers of human souls.' There were two main problems. The first was that many people did not want their souls to be engineered, thank you very much. They were content with their souls being left as they were when they had come into this world; and when you tried to lead them, they resisted. Come to this free open-air concert, comrade. Oh, we really think you should attend. Yes, of course it is voluntary, but it might be a mistake if you didn't show your face . . .

And the second problem with engineering human souls was more basic. It was this: who engineers the engineers?

He remembered an open-air concert at a park in Kharkov. His First Symphony had set all the neighbourhood dogs barking. The crowd laughed, the orchestra played louder, the dogs yapped all the more, the audience laughed all the more. Now, his music had set bigger dogs barking. History was repeating itself: the first time as farce, the second time as tragedy.

He did not want to make himself into a dramatic character. But sometimes, as his mind skittered in the small hours, he thought: so this is what history has come to. All that striving and idealism and hope and progress and science and art and conscience, and it all ends like this, with a man standing by a lift, at his feet a small case containing cigarettes, underwear and tooth powder; standing there and waiting to be taken away.

He forced his mind across to a different composer with a different travelling case. Prokofiev had left Russia for the West shortly after the Revolution; he returned for the first time in 1927. He was a sophisticated man, Sergei Sergeyevich, with expensive tastes. Also a Christian Scientist – not that this was relevant to the story. The customs officers at the Soviet border were not sophisticated; further, their minds were filled with notions of sabotage and spies and counter-revolution. They opened Prokofiev's suitcase and found on the top an item which baffled them: a pair of pyjamas. They unfolded them, held them up, turned them this way and that, looking at one another in astonishment. Perhaps Sergei Sergeyevich was embarrassed. At any rate, he left the explaining to his wife. But Ptashka, after their years in exile, had forgotten the Russian word for night-blouse. The problem was eventually resolved by dumbshow, and the couple were allowed through. But somehow, the incident was entirely typical of Prokofiev.

His scrapbook. What kind of a man buys a scrapbook and then fills it with insulting articles about himself? A madman? An ironist? A Russian? He thought of Gogol, standing in front of a mirror and from time to time calling out his own name, in a tone of revulsion and alienation. This did not seem to him the act of a madman.

His official status was that of a 'non-Party Bolshevik'. Stalin liked to say that the finest quality of the Bolshevik was modesty. Yes, and Russia was the homeland of elephants.

When Galina was born, he and Nita used to joke about christening her Sumburina. It meant Little Muddle. Muddlikins. It would have been an act of ironic bravado. No, of suicidal folly.

Tukhachevsky's letter to Stalin received no answer. Dmitri Dmitrievich himself did not follow the advice of Platon

Kerzhentsev. He made no public statement, no apology for the excesses of youth, no recantation; though he withdrew his Fourth Symphony, which to those without ears to hear would assuredly sound like a medley of quacks and grunts and growls. Meanwhile, all his operas and ballets were removed from the repertoire. His career had simply stopped.

And then, in the spring of 1937, he had his First Conversation with Power. Of course, he had talked to Power before, or Power had talked to him: officials, bureaucrats, politicians, coming with suggestions, proposals, ultimata. Power had talked to him through newspapers, publicly, and had whispered in his ear, privately. Recently, Power had humiliated him, taken away his livelihood, ordered him to repent. Power had told him how it wanted him to work, how it wanted him to live. Now it was hinting that perhaps, on consideration, it might not want him to live any more. Power had decided to have a face-to-face with him. Power's name was Zakrevsky, and Power, as it expressed itself to people like him in Leningrad, resided in the Big House. Many who went into the Big House on Liteiny Prospekt never emerged again.

He had been given an appointment for a Saturday morning. He maintained to family and friends that it was doubtless all a formality, perhaps an automatic consequence of the continuing articles against him in *Pravda*. He barely believed this himself, and doubted they did. Not many were summoned to the Big House to discuss musical theory. He was, of course, punctual. And Power was at first correct and polite. Zakrevsky asked about his work, how his professional affairs were proceeding, what he intended to compose next. In reply, he mentioned, almost as a reflex, that he was preparing a symphony on the subject of Lenin – which might conceivably have been the case. He then thought it sensible to refer to the press campaign against him, and was encouraged by the interrogator's almost perfunctory dismissal of such matters. Next he was asked about his friends, and whom he saw on a regular basis. He did not know how to answer such questions. Zakrevsky helped him along.

'You are, I understand, acquainted with Marshal Tukhachevsky?'

'Yes, I know him.'

'Tell me about how you made his acquaintance.'

He recalled the meeting backstage at the Small Hall in Moscow. He explained that the Marshal was a well-known music lover who had attended many of his concerts, who played the violin, and even made violins as a hobby. The Marshal had invited him to his apartment; they had even played music together. He was a good amateur violinist. Did he mean 'good'? Capable, certainly. And, yes, capable of improvement.

But Zakrevsky was uninterested in how far the Marshal's fingering and bow technique had progressed.

'You went to his home on many occasions?'

'From time to time, yes.'

'From time to time over a period of how many years? Eight, nine, ten?'

'Yes, that is probably the case.'

'So, let us say, four or five visits a year? Forty or fifty in total?'

'Fewer, I would say. I have never counted. But fewer.'

'But you are an intimate friend of Marshal Tukhachevsky?'

He paused for thought. 'No, not an intimate friend, but a good friend.'

He did not mention the Marshal arranging financial

support for him; advising him; writing to Stalin on his behalf. Either Zakrevsky would know this, or he wouldn't.

'And who else was present at these forty or fifty occasions at the home of your good friend?'

'Not so many. Only members of the family.'

'Only members of the family?' The interrogator's tone was rightly sceptical.

'And musicians. And musicologists.'

'Any politicians there, by any chance?'

'No, no politicians.'

'You are quite sure about that?'

'Well, you see, they were sometimes rather crowded gatherings. And I did not exactly . . . In point of fact, I was often playing the piano . . .'

'And what did you talk about?'

'About music.'

'And politics.'

'No.'

'Come, come, how could anyone fail to talk about politics with Marshal Tukhachevsky of all people?'

'He was, shall we say, off duty. Among friends and musicians.'

'And were there any other off-duty politicians present?'

'No, never. There was never any talk of politics in my presence.'

The interrogator looked at him for a long while. Then came a change of voice, as if to prepare him for the seriousness and menace of his position.

'Now, I think you should try to shake your memory. It cannot be that you were at the home of Marshal Tukhachevsky, in your capacity as a "good friend" as you put it, on a regular basis over the last ten years and that you did not talk about politics. For instance, the plot to assassinate Comrade Stalin. What did you hear about that?'

At which point, he knew that he was a dead man. 'And yet another's hour is near at hand' – and this time it was his. He reiterated, as plainly as he could, that there had never been any talk of politics at Marshal Tukhachevsky's; they were purely musical evenings; matters of state were left at the door with hats and coats. He was not sure if this was the best phrase. But Zakrevsky was barely listening.

'Then I suggest you think a little harder,' the interrogator told him. 'Some of the other guests have verified the plot already.'

He realised that Tukhachevsky must have been arrested, that the Marshal's career was over, and his life as well; that the investigation was just beginning, and that all those around the Marshal would soon vanish from the face of the earth. His own innocence was irrelevant. The truth of his answers was irrelevant. What had been decided had been decided. And if they needed to show that the conspiracy which they had either just discovered or just invented was so perniciously widespread that even the country's most famous – if recently disgraced – composer was involved, then that was what they would show. Which explained the matter-of-factness in Zakrevsky's tone as he brought the interview to a close.

'Very well. Today is Saturday. It is twelve o'clock now, and you can go. But I will only give you forty-eight hours. On Monday at twelve o'clock you will without fail remember everything. You must recall every detail of all the discussions regarding the plot against Comrade Stalin, of which you were one of the chief witnesses.'

★

He was a dead man. He told Nita all that had been said, and he saw beneath her reassurances that she agreed he was a dead man. He knew he must protect those closest around him, and to do so needed to be calm, but could only be frantic. He burnt anything that might be incriminating – except that once you had been labelled an enemy of the people and the associate of a known assassin, everything around you became incriminating. He might as well burn the whole apartment. He feared for Nita, for his mother, for Galya, for anyone who had ever entered or left his apartment.

'There is no escaping one's destiny.' And so, he would be dead at thirty. Older than Pergolesi, true, but younger even than Schubert. And Pushkin himself, for that matter. His name and his music would be obliterated. Not only would he not exist, he would never have existed. He had been a mistake, swiftly corrected; a face in a photograph that went missing the next time that photograph was printed. And even if, at some point in the future, he was disinterred, what would they find? Four symphonies, one piano concerto, some orchestral suites, two pieces for string quartet but not a single finished quartet, some piano music, a cello sonata, two operas, some film and ballet music. He would be remembered by what? The opera which had brought him disgrace, the symphony he had wisely withdrawn? Perhaps his First Symphony would make the cheerful prelude to concerts of mature works by composers lucky enough to outlive him.

But even this was false comfort, he realised. What he himself thought was irrelevant. The future would decide what the future would decide. For instance, that his music was quite unimportant. That he might have come to something as a composer if he had not, through vanity, involved himself in a treasonous plot against the head of state. Who could tell what the future would believe? We expect too much of the future – hoping that it will quarrel with the present. And who could tell what shadow his death would cast on his family. He imagined Galya emerging at sixteen from her Siberian orphanage, believing that her parents had heartlessly abandoned her, unaware that her father had written even a single note of music.

When the threats against him had first begun, he told friends: 'Even if they cut off both my hands, I shall continue to write music with a pen in my mouth.' They had been words of defiance intended to keep up everyone's spirits, his own included. But they did not want to cut off his hands, his small, 'non-pianistic' hands. They might want to torture him, and he would agree to everything they said immediately, as he had no capacity for bearing pain. Names would be put in front of him, and he would implicate all of them. No, he would say briefly, which would quickly change to Yes, Yes, Yes and Yes. Yes, I was there at the time in the Marshal's apartment; Yes I heard him say whatever you suggest he might have said; Yes this general and that politician were involved in the plot, I saw and heard it for myself. But there would be no melodramatic cutting-off of his hands, just a businesslike bullet to the back of the head.

Those words of his had been at best a foolish boast, at worst a mere figure of speech. And Power had no interest in figures of speech. Power knew only facts, and its language consisted of phrases and euphemisms designed either to publicise or to conceal those facts. There were no composers writing with a pen between their teeth in Stalin's Russia. From now on there would be only two types of composer: those who were alive and frightened; and those who were dead.

★

How recently he had sensed within him youth's indestructibility. More than that – its incorruptibility. And beyond that, beneath it all, a conviction of the rightness and truth of whatever talent he had, and whatever music he had written. All this was not in any way undermined. It was just, now, completely irrelevant.

On the Saturday night, and again on the Sunday night, he drank himself to sleep. It was not a complicated matter. He had a light head, and a couple of glasses of vodka would often make him need to lie down. This weakness was also an advantage. Drink, and then rest, while others carried on drinking. This left you fresher the next morning, better able to work.

Anapa had been famous as a centre of the Grape Cure. He had once joked to Tanya that he preferred the Vodka Cure. And so, now, on perhaps the last two nights of his life, he took the cure.

On that Monday morning he kissed Nita, held Galya one last time, and caught the bus to the dismal grey building on Liteiny Prospekt. He was always punctual, and would go to his death being punctual. He gazed briefly at the River Neva, which would outlast them all. At the Big House he presented himself to the guard at reception. The soldier looked through his roster but could not find the name. He was asked to repeat it. He did so. The soldier went down the list again.

'What is your business? Who have you come to see?'

'Interrogator Zakrevsky.'

The soldier nodded slowly. Then, without looking up,

said, 'Well, you can go home. You are not on the list. Zakrevsky isn't coming in today, so there is nobody to receive you.'

Thus ended his First Conversation with Power.

He went home. He assumed it must be some trick – they were letting him go so they could follow him and then arrest all his friends and associates. But it turned out to have been a sudden piece of luck in his life. Between the Saturday and the Monday, Zakrevsky had himself fallen under suspicion. His interrogator interrogated. His arrester arrested.

Still, if his dismissal from the Big House was not a trick, it could only be a bureaucratic delay. They were hardly likely to give up their pursuit of Tukhachevsky; so Zakrevsky's departure was only a temporary hitch. Some new Zakrevsky would be appointed and the summons would be renewed.

Three weeks after the Marshal's arrest he was shot, together with the elite of the Red Army. The generals' plot to assassinate Comrade Stalin had been discovered just in time. Among those in Tukhachevsky's immediate entourage to be arrested and shot was their mutual friend Nikolai Sergeyevich Zhilyayev, the distinguished musicologist. Perhaps there was a musicologists' plot waiting to be uncovered, followed by a composers' plot and a trombonists' plot. Why not? 'Nothing but madness in the world.'

It seemed such a brief while ago that they were all laughing at Professor Nikolayev's definition of a musicologist. Imagine we are eating scrambled eggs, the Professor used to say. My cook, Pasha, has prepared them, and you and I are eating them. Along comes a man who has not prepared them and is not eating them, but he talks about them as if he knows everything about them – *that* is a musicologist.

But it did not seem so funny now that they were shooting even musicologists. Nikolai Sergeyevich Zhilyayev's crimes were given as monarchism, terrorism and spying.

And so he began his vigils by the lift. He was not unique in this. Others across the city did the same, wanting to spare those they loved the spectacle of their arrest. Each night he followed the same routine: he evacuated his bowels, kissed his sleeping daughter, kissed his wakeful wife, took the small case from her hands, and closed the front door. Almost as if he was going off for the night shift. Which in a way he was. And then he stood and waited, thinking about the past, fearing for the future, smoking his way through the brief present. The case resting against his calf was there to reassure him, and to reassure others; a practical measure. It made him look as if he were in charge of events rather than a victim of them. Men who left home with a case in their hands traditionally returned. Men dragged from their beds in their night-clothes often did not. Whether or not this was true was unimportant. What mattered was this: it looked as if he was not afraid.

This was one of the questions in his head: was it brave to be standing there waiting for them, or was it cowardly? Or was it neither – merely sensible? He did not expect to discover the answer.

★

Would Zakrevsky's successor begin as Zakrevsky had, with courteous preliminaries, then a hardening, a threat, and an invitation to return with a list of names? But what additional evidence could they need against Tukhachevsky, given that he had already been tried, condemned and executed? More likely, it would be part of a wider investigation into the Marshal's outer circle of friends, the inner circle having been dealt with. He would be asked about his political convictions, his family and his professional connections. Well, he could remember himself as a boy standing in front of the apartment building on Nikolayevskaya Street, proudly wearing a red ribbon on his coat; later, rushing with a group of schoolfellows to the Finland Station to greet Lenin on his return to Russia. His earliest compositions, predating his official Opus One, had been a 'Funeral March for the Victims of the Revolution', and a 'Hymn to Liberty'.

But proceed any further, and facts were no longer facts, merely statements open to divergent interpretation. So, he had been at school with the children of Kerensky and Trotsky: once a matter of pride, then of interest, now, perhaps, of silent shame. So, his uncle Maxim Lavrentyevich Kostrikin, an old Bolshevik exiled to Siberia for his part in the 1905 Revolution, had been the first encourager of his nephew's revolutionary sympathies. But Old Bolsheviks, once a pride and a blessing, were nowadays more frequently a curse.

He had never joined the Party – and never would. He could not join a party which killed: it was as simple as that. But as a 'non-Party Bolshevik' he had allowed himself to be portrayed as fully supportive of the Party. He had written music for films and ballets and oratorios which glorified the Revolution and all its works. His Second Symphony had been a cantata celebrating the tenth anniversary of the Revolution, in which he had set some quite disgusting verses by Alexander Bezymensky. He had written scores applauding collectivisation and denouncing sabotage in industry. His music for the film *Counterplan* – about a group of factory workers who spontaneously devise a scheme to boost production – had been a tremendous success. 'The Song of the Counterplan' had been whistled and hummed all over the country, and still was. Currently – perhaps always, and certainly for as long as was necessary – he was at work on a symphony dedicated to the memory of Lenin.

He doubted any of this would convince Zakrevsky's replacement. Did any part of him believe in Communism? Certainly, if the alternative was Fascism. But he did not believe in Utopia, in the perfectibility of mankind, in the engineering of the human soul. After five years of Lenin's New Economic Policy, he had written to a friend that 'Heaven on Earth will come in 200,000,000,000 years.' But that, he now thought, might have been over-optimistic.

Theories were clean and convincing and comprehensible. Life was messy and full of nonsense. He had put the theory of Free Love into practice, first with Tanya, then with Nita. Indeed, with both of them at the same time; they had overlapped in his heart, and sometimes still did. It had been a slow and painful business, discovering that the theory of love did not match the reality of life. It was like expecting to be able to write a symphony because you had once read a handbook of composition. And on top of this, he himself was weak-willed and indecisive – except on those occasions when he was strong-willed and decisive. But even then he didn't necessarily make the right decisions. So his emotional life had been . . .

how best to sum it up? He smiled ruefully to himself. Yes indeed: muddle instead of music.

He had wanted Tanya; his mother had disapproved. He had wanted Nina; his mother had disapproved. He had hidden their marriage from her for several weeks, not wanting their first happiness to be clouded with ill feeling. This had not been the most heroic action of his life, he admitted. And when he did confess the news, his mother reacted as if she'd known all along – perhaps she had read the registrar's diary – and saw no reason to approve. She had a way of talking about Nina which sounded like praise yet was in fact criticism. Perhaps, after his death, which could not be far away, they would form a household together. Mother, daughter-in-law, granddaughter: three generations of women. Such households were increasingly common in Russia these days.

He may have got things wrong; but he was not a fool, nor altogether naive. He had been conscious from the beginning that it was necessary to render unto Caesar that which was Caesar's. So why was Caesar angry with him? No one could say he was not productive: he wrote quickly, and rarely missed a deadline. He could turn out efficiently tuneful music which pleased him for a month and the public for a decade. But this was precisely the point. Caesar didn't just demand that tribute be rendered unto him; he also nominated the currency in which it should be paid. Why, Comrade Shostakovich, does your new symphony not sound like your wonderful 'Song of the Counterplan'? Why is the weary steel-worker not whistling its first theme on his way home? We know, Comrade Shostakovich, that you are well capable of writing music which pleases the masses. So why do you persist with your formalist quacks and grunts which the smug bourgeoisie who still command the concert halls merely pretend to admire?

Yes, he had been naive about Caesar. Or rather, he had been working from an outdated model. In the old days, Caesar had demanded tribute money, a sum to acknowledge his power, a certain percentage of your calculated worth. But things had moved on, and the new Caesars of the Kremlin had upgraded the system: nowadays your tribute money was calculated at the full 100% of your worth. Or, if possible, more.

When he was a student – those years of cheerfulness, hope and invulnerability – he had slaved for three years as a cinema pianist. He had accompanied the screen at the Piccadilly on Nevsky Prospekt; also at the Bright Reel and the Splendid Palace. It was hard, demeaning work; some of the proprietors were skinflints who would sack you rather than pay your wages. Still, he used to remind himself that Brahms had played the piano at a sailors' brothel in Hamburg. Which might have beem more fun, admittedly.

He tried to watch the screen above him and play appropriate music. The audience preferred the old romantic tunes which were familiar to them; but often, he would get bored, and then play his own compositions. These did not go down so well. In the cinema, it was the opposite from the concert hall: audiences would applaud when they disapproved of something. One evening, while accompanying a film called *Marsh and Water Birds of Sweden*, he found himself in a more than usually satirical mood. First he began to imitate bird calls on the piano, and then, as the marsh and water birds flew higher and higher, the piano worked itself up into a greater and greater passion. There was loud applause, which in his naivety he took to be aimed at the ridiculous film; and so he played all the harder. Afterwards, the audience had complained to the cinema manager: the pianist must have been drunk, what he played was never music, he had insulted the beautiful film and also its audience. The manager had sacked him.

And that, he now realised, had been his career in miniature: hard work, some success, a failure to respect musical norms, official disapproval, suspension of pay, the sack. Except that now he was in the grown-up world, where the sack meant something much more final.

He imagined his mother sitting in a cinema while pictures of his girlfriends were projected on to the screen. Tanya – his mother applauds. Nina – his mother applauds. Rozaliya – his mother applauds even harder. Cleopatra, the Venus de Milo, the Queen of Sheba – his mother, ever unimpressed, continues to applaud unsmilingly.

His nocturnal vigils lasted for ten days. Nita argued – not from evidence, more from optimism and determination – that the immediate danger had probably passed. Neither of them believed this, but he was weary of standing, of waiting for the lift's machinery to grind and whirr. He was weary of his own fear. And so he returned to lying in the dark fully clothed, his wife at his side, his overnight bag next to the bed. A few feet away Galya would be sleeping as an infant does, careless about matters of state.

And then, one morning, he picked up his case and opened it. He put his underclothes back in the drawer, his toothbrush and tooth powder in the bathroom cabinet, and his three packets of Kazbeki on his desk.

And he waited for Power to resume its conversation with him. But he never heard from the Big House again.

Not that Power was idle. Many of those around him began to disappear, some to camps, some to execution. His mother-in-law, his brother-in-law, his Old Bolshevik uncle, associates, a former lover. And what of Zakrevsky, who had not come into work that fatal Monday? No one ever heard from him again. Perhaps Zakrevsky had never really existed.

But there is no escaping one's destiny; and his, for the moment, was apparently to live. To live and to work. There would be no rest. 'We rest only when we dream,' as Blok put it; though at this time most people's dreams were not restful. But life continued; soon Nita was pregnant again, and soon he began adding to the opus numbers he had feared would end with the Fourth Symphony.

His Fifth, which he wrote that summer, was premiered in November 1937 in the Hall of the Leningrad Philharmonic. An elderly philologist told Glikman that only once before in his lifetime had he witnessed such a vast and insistent ovation: forty-four years previously, when Tchaikovsky had conducted the premiere of his Sixth Symphony. A journalist – foolish? hopeful? sympathetic? – described the Fifth as 'A Soviet Artist's Creative Reply to Just Criticism'. He never repudiated the phrase; and many came to believe it was to be found in his own hand at the head of the score. These words turned out to be the most famous he ever wrote – or rather, never wrote. He allowed them to stand because they protected his music. Let Power have the words, because words cannot stain music. Music escapes from words: that is its purpose, and its majesty.

The phrase also permitted those with asses' ears to hear in his symphony what they wanted to hear. They missed the screeching irony of the final movement, that mockery of triumph. They heard only triumph itself, some loyal endorsement of Soviet music, Soviet musicology, of life under the sun of Stalin's constitution. He had ended the symphony fortissimo and in the major. What if he had ended it pianissimo and in the minor? On such things might a life – might several lives – turn. Well, 'Nothing but nonsense in the world.'

The Fifth Symphony's success was instant and universal. Such a sudden phenomenon was accordingly analysed by Party bureaucrats and tame musicologists, who came up with an official description of the work, to assist the Soviet public's understanding. They called his Fifth 'an optimistic tragedy'.

2: On the Plane

All he knew was that *this* was the worst time.

One fear drives out another, as one nail drives out another. So, as the climbing plane seemed to hit solid ledges of air, he concentrated on the local, immediate fear: of immolation, disintegration, instant oblivion. Fear normally drives out all other emotions as well; but not shame. Fear and shame swilled happily together in his stomach.

He could see the wing and a churning propeller of the American Overseas Airlines plane; that, and the clouds they were heading into. Other members of the delegation, with better seats and greater curiosity, were pressing against the little windows for a last glimpse of the New York skyline. The six of them were in celebratory mood, he could hear, and eager for the stewardess to come round with the first offer of drinks. They would toast the great success of the congress, and assure one another that it was precisely because they had advanced the cause of Peace so much that the warmongering State Department had revoked their visas and packed them home early. He was just as keen on the stewardess and the drinks, if for different reasons. He wanted to forget everything that had happened. He drew the patterned curtains across the window, as if to blot out the memory. Small chance of that, however much he drank.

'There is only good vodka and very good vodka – there is no such thing as bad vodka.' This was the wisdom from Moscow to Leningrad, from Arkhangelsk to Kuibyshev. But there was also American vodka, which, he had now learnt, was ritually improved with fruit flavours, with lemon and ice and tonic water, its taste covered up in cocktails. So perhaps there might be such a thing as bad vodka.

During the war, anxious before a long journey, he would sometimes go for a session of hypnotherapy. He wished he'd had a treatment before the outbound flight, then one each day of their week in New York, and another before the return journey. Or better still, they could have just put him in a wooden crate with a week's supply of sausage and vodka, dumped it at LaGuardia airport and loaded it back on the plane for their return. So, Dmitri Dmitrievich, how was your trip? Wonderful, thank you, I saw all I wished to see and the company was most agreeable.

On the flight out, the seat beside him had been occupied by his official protector, warder, translator and new best friend as of twenty-four hours previously. Who naturally smoked Belomory. When they were handed menus in English and French, he had asked his companion for a translation. On the right were cocktails and alcoholic drinks and cigarettes. On the left, he had assumed, was food. No, came the reply, these were other things you could order. A bureaucratic forefinger ran down the list. Dominoes, checkers, dice, backgammon. Newspapers, stationery, magazines, postcards. Electric razor, ice bag, sewing kit, medical kit, chewing gum, tooth-brushes, Kleenex.

'And that?' he had asked, pointing at the only untranslated item.

A stewardess was called, and a long explanation followed. Eventually, he was told,

'Benzedrine inhaler.'

'Benzedrine inhaler?'

'For drug-addict capitalists who shit themselves on take-off and landing,' said his new best friend, with a certain ideological smugness.

He himself suffered from non-capitalist fear on take-off and landing. Had he not known it would go immediately into his official file, he might have tried this decadent Western invention.

Fear: what did those who inflicted it know? They knew that it worked, even how it worked, but not what it felt like. 'The wolf cannot speak of the fear of the sheep,' as they say. While he had been awaiting orders from the Big House in St Leninsburg, Oistrakh had been expecting arrest in Moscow. The violinist had described to him how, night after night, they came for someone in his apartment block. Never a mass arrest; just one victim, and then the next night another – a system which ramped up the fear for those who remained, who had temporarily survived. Eventually, all the tenants had been taken except for those in his apartment and the one opposite. The next night the police van arrived again, they heard the downstairs door slam, footsteps coming along the corridor . . . and going to the other apartment. From this exact point, Oistrakh said, he was always afraid; and would be, he knew, for the rest of his life.

★

Now, on the flight back, his minder left him alone. It would be thirty hours before they reached Moscow, with stops at Newfoundland, Reykjavik, Frankfurt and Berlin. It would be comfortable at least: the seats were good, the noise level bearable, the stewardesses well groomed. They brought food served on china and linen with heavy cutlery. Enormous shrimps, fat and sleek like politicians, swimming in shrimp-cocktail sauce. A steak, almost as tall as it was wide, with mushrooms and potatoes and green beans. Fruit salad. He ate, but mainly he drank. He no longer had the light head of his younger days. One Scotch and soda followed another, but they failed to put him out. No one stopped him, neither the airline nor his companions, who were audibly merry, and probably drinking just as much. Then, after coffee had been served, the cabin seemed to grow warmer, and everyone dropped off to sleep, himself included.

What had he hoped of America? He had hoped to meet Stravinsky. Even though he knew it was a dream, indeed a fantasy. He had always revered Stravinsky's music. He'd barely missed a performance of *Petrushka* at the Mariinsky. He'd played second piano in the Russian premiere of *Les Noces*, performed the Serenade in A in public, transcribed the *Symphony of Psalms* for four hands. If there was a single composer of the twentieth century who might be called great, it was Stravinsky. The *Symphony of Psalms* was one of the most brilliant works in musical history. All this, without doubt or hesitation, he declared to be the case.

But Stravinsky would not be there. He had sent a snubbing and well-publicised telegram: 'Regret not being able to join welcomers of Soviet artists coming this country. But all my ethic and esthetic convictions oppose such gesture.'

★

And what had he expected of America? Certainly not cartoon capitalists in stovepipe hats and Stars and Stripes waistcoats marching down Fifth Avenue and trampling underfoot the starving proletariat. Any more than he expected a trumpeted land of freedom – he doubted such a place existed anywhere. Perhaps he had imagined a combination of technological advancement, social conformity, and the sober manners of a pioneering nation come into wealth. Ilf and Petrov, after taking a road-trip across the country, had written that thinking about America made them melancholy, while having the opposite effect on Americans themselves. They also reported that Americans, contrary to their own propaganda, were very passive by nature, since everything was pre-processed for them, from ideas to food. Even the cows standing motionless in the fields looked like advertisements for condensed milk.

His first surprise had been the behaviour of American journalists. There had been an advance guard of them at Frankfurt airport on the journey out, waiting in ambush. They bawled questions and shoved cameras into his face. There had been a cheerful rudeness about them, an assumption of superior values. The fact that they couldn't pronounce your name was your name's fault, not theirs. So they shortened it.

'Hey, Shosti, look this way! Wave your hat at us!'

That had been later, at LaGuardia airport. Dutifully, he had raised his hat and waved it, as had his fellow delegates.

'Hey, Shosti, give us a smile!'

'Hey, Shosti, how do you like America?'

'Hey, Shosti, do you prefer blondes or brunettes?'

Yes, they had even asked him that. If at home you were spied on by the men who smoked Belomory, here in America you were spied on by the press. After their plane had landed, a journalist had got hold of a stewardess and quizzed her about the behaviour of the Soviet delegation during the flight. She reported that they had chatted to their fellow passengers, and enjoyed drinking dry martinis and Scotch and soda. And such information was duly printed in the *New York Times* as if it were of interest!

Good things first. His suitcase was full of gramophone records and American cigarettes. He had heard the Juilliards perform three Bartok quartets and had met them backstage afterwards. He had heard the New York Philharmonic under Stokowski in a programme of Panufnik, Virgil Thomson, Sibelius, Khachaturian and Brahms. He had himself played – with his small, 'non-pianistic' hands – the second movement of his Fifth Symphony at Madison Square Garden in front of 15,000 people. Their applause was thunderous, unstoppable, competitive. Well, America was the land of competition, so perhaps they wanted to prove they could clap longer and louder than Russian audiences. It had embarrassed him and – who knew? – perhaps the State Department as well. He had met some American artists who had received him most cordially: Aaron Copland, Clifford Odets, Arthur Miller, a young writer called Mailer. He had received a large scroll thanking him for his visit, signed by forty-two musicians from Artie Shaw to Bruno Walter. And there the good things ended. These had been his spoonfuls of honey in a barrel of tar.

He had hoped for some obscurity among the hundreds of other participants, but found to his dismay that he was the star name of the Soviet delegation. He had given a short speech on the Friday night and an immense one on the Saturday night. He had answered questions and posed for photographs. He was treated well; it was a public success – and also the greatest humiliation of his life. He felt nothing but self-disgust and self-contempt. It had been the perfect trap, the more so because the two parts of it were not connected. Communists at one end, capitalists at the other, himself in the middle. And nothing to do except scuttle through the brightly lit corridors of some experiment, as a series of doors opened in front of him and closed immediately behind him.

And it had all started again because of another trip Stalin had made to the opera. How ironic was that? The fact that it was not even his opera, but Muradeli's, made absolutely no difference, neither at the end, nor indeed from the beginning. Naturally enough, it had been a leap year: 1948.

It was a commonplace to say that tyranny turned the world upside down; and yet it was true. In the twelve years between 1936 and 1948, he had never felt safer than during the Great Patriotic War. A disaster to the rescue, as they say. Millions upon millions died, but at least suffering became more general, and in that lay his temporary salvation. Because, though tyranny might be paranoid, it was not necessarily stupid. If it were stupid, it would not survive; just as if it had principles, it would not survive. Tyranny understood how some parts – the weak parts – of most people worked. It had spent years killing priests and closing churches, but if soldiers fought more stubbornly under the blessing of priests, then priests would be brought back for their short-term usefulness. And if in wartime people needed music to keep their spirits up, then composers would be put to work as well.

If the state made concessions, so did its citizens. He made political speeches written for him by others, but – so upside down had the world become – they were speeches whose sentiments, if not whose language, he could actually endorse. He spoke at an anti-Fascist meeting of artists about 'our gigantic battle with German vandalism', and 'the mission to liberate mankind from the brown plague'. 'Everything for the Front,' he had urged, sounding like Power itself. He was confident, fluent, convincing. 'Soon, happier times will come,' he promised his fellow-artists, parroting Stalin.

The brown plague included Wagner – a composer who had always been put to work by Power. In and out of fashion all century, according to the politics of the day. When the Molotov–Ribbentrop Pact was signed, Mother Russia had embraced its new Fascist ally as a middle-aged widow embraces a husky young neighbour, the more enthusiastically for the passion coming late, and against all reason. Wagner became a great composer again, and Eisenstein was ordered to direct *The Valkyrie* at the Bolshoi. Less than two years later, Hitler invaded Russia, and Wagner reverted to being a vile Fascist, a piece of brown scum.

★

All of which had been a dark comedy; though one which obscured the more important question. Pushkin had put the words into Mozart's mouth:

> Genius and evil
> Are two things incompatible. You agree?

For himself, he agreed. Wagner had a mean soul, and it showed. He was evil in his anti-Semitism and his other racial attitudes. Therefore he could not be a genius, for all the burnish and glitter of his music.

He had spent much of the war in Kuibyshev with his family. They were safe there, and once his mother was out of Leningrad and able to join them, he became less anxious. Also, there were fewer cats sharpening their claws on his soul. Of course, as a patriotic member of the Union of Composers, he was often required in Moscow. He would pack enough garlic sausage and vodka to last the journey. 'The best bird is the sausage,' as they said in the Ukraine. The trains would stop for hours, sometimes days; you never knew when sudden troop movements or a lack of coal would interrupt your journey.

He travelled soft class, which was just as well, as the carriages of hard class were like wards of potential typhus cases. To prevent infection, he wore an amulet of garlic around his neck, and another around each wrist. 'The smell will put off girls,' he would explain, 'but such sacrifices have to be made in wartime.'

Once, he had been travelling back from Moscow with . . . no, he couldn't recall. A couple of days out, the train had stopped on some long, dusty platform. They had opened the window and poked their heads out. The early-morning sun was in their eyes and the filthy song of some raucous beggar in their ears. Had they given him some sausage? Vodka? A few kopecks? Why did he half-remember this station, this beggar among thousands of others? Was it to do with a joke? Had one of them made a joke? But which one? No, it was no good.

He couldn't bring to mind the beggar's barrack-room obscenities. What came back to him instead was a soldiers' song from the previous century. He didn't know the tune, just the words he'd once found, glancing through Turgenev's letters:

> Russia, my cherished mother,
> She doesn't take anything by force;
> She only takes things willingly surrendered
> While holding a knife to your throat.

Turgenev was not to his literary taste: too civilised, not fantastical enough. He preferred Pushkin and Chekhov, and Gogol best of all. But even Turgenev, for all his faults, had a true Russian pessimism. Indeed, he understood that to be Russian was to be pessimistic. He had also written that, however much you scrubbed a Russian, he would always remain a Russian. That was what Karlo-Marlo and their descendants had never understood. They wanted to be engineers of human souls; but Russians, for all their faults, were not machines. So it was not really engineering they were up to, but scrubbing. Scrub, scrub, scrub, let's wash away all this old Russianness and paint a shiny new Sovietness on top. But it never worked – the paint began to flake off almost as soon as it was applied.

To be Russian was to be pessimistic; to be Soviet was to be optimistic. That was why the words *Soviet Russia* were a contradiction in terms. Power had never understood this. It thought that if you killed off enough of the population, and fed the rest a diet of propaganda and terror, then optimism would result. But where was the logic in that? Just as they had kept on telling him, in various ways and words, through musical bureaucrats and newspaper editorials, that what they wanted was 'an optimistic Shostakovich'. Another contradiction in terms.

One of the few places where optimism and pessimism could happily coexist – indeed, where the presence of both is necessary for survival – was family life. So, for instance, he loved Nita (optimism), but did not know if he was a good husband (pessimism). He was an anxious man, and aware that anxiety makes people egotistical and bad company. Nita would go off to work; but the moment she arrived at her Institute, he would telephone to ask when she was coming home. He could see that this was annoying; but his anxiety would just get the better of him.

He loved his children (optimism), but was not sure if he was a good father (pessimism). Sometimes he felt his love for his children was abnormal, even morbid. Well, life is not a walk across a field, as the saying goes.

Galya and Maxim were taught never to lie, and always to be polite. He insisted on good manners. He explained to Maxim at an early age that you preceded a woman upstairs but followed her downstairs. When the two of them acquired bicycles, he made them learn the highway code, and practise it even when riding on the emptiest forest path: left arm out to indicate left turn, right arm out to indicate right turn. At Kuibyshev he also supervised their gymnastic exercises each morning. He would turn on the radio, and all three would follow the hearty-voiced instructions of a fellow called Gordeyev. 'That's right! Feet shoulder-width apart! First exercise . . .' And so on.

Apart from these parental physical jerks, he did not train his body; he merely inhabited it. A friend had once shown him what he called gymnastics for the intelligentsia. You took a box of matches and threw its contents on the floor, then bent down and picked them up, one by one. The first time he tried it himself, he lost patience and stuffed all the matches back in handfuls. He persevered, but the next time, just as he was bending down, the telephone went, and he was needed at once; so the housekeeper was detailed to pick up the matches instead.

Nita loved skiing and mountaineering; he was put in a state of mortal fear as soon as he felt the treacherous snow beneath his skis. She enjoyed boxing matches; he could not bear the sight of one man beating another nearly to death. He even failed to master the form of exercise closest to his own art: dancing. He could write a polka, he could play one jauntily on the piano, but put him on the dance floor and his feet would be ineptly disobedient.

What he enjoyed was playing patience, which calmed him; or card games with friends, as long as they played for money. And though he was neither robust nor coordinated enough for sport, he liked umpiring. Before the war, in Leningrad, he had qualified as a football referee. During their exile in Kuibyshev, he organised and umpired volleyball competitions. He would announce solemnly, in one of the few English phrases he had somehow picked up, 'It is time to play volleyball.' And then add, in Russian, a sports commentator's favourite phrase: 'The match will take place whatever the weather.'

Galya and Maxim were rarely punished. If they did anything naughty or dishonest, this immediately reduced their parents to a state of extreme anxiety. Nita would frown and look at the children reproachfully; he would light cigarette after cigarette while pacing up and down. This dumbshow of anguish was often chastisement enough for the children. Besides, the whole country was a punishment cell: why introduce a child so early to what it would see quite enough of in its lifetime?

Still, there were occasionally cases of extreme naughtiness. Once, Maxim had faked a bicycle accident, pretending to be hurt, perhaps even unconscious, only to jump up and start laughing when he saw how distraught his parents were. In such cases he would say to Maxim (for it usually was Maxim), 'Please come and see me in my study. I need to have a serious talk with you.' And even these words brought a kind of pain to the boy. In his study, he would make Maxim write down a description of what he had done, followed by a promise never to behave like that again, then sign and date this affidavit. If Maxim repeated his sin, he would summon the boy to his study, take the written promise from the desk drawer, and make Maxim read it aloud. Though the boy's shame was often such that it felt as if the punishment were being visited back upon the father.

★

His best memories of wartime exile were simple ones: he and Galya playing with a litter of pigs, trying to hold on to the snorting, bristly bundles of flesh; or Maxim doing his famous impression of a Bulgarian policeman tying his bootlaces. They spent summers on a former estate at Ivanovo, where Poultry Collective Farm Number 69 became an ad hoc House of Composers. Here he wrote his Eighth Symphony on a desk consisting of a piece of board nailed to the inside wall of a converted henhouse. He could always work, regardless of chaos and discomfort around him. This was his salvation. Others were distracted by the sounds of normal life. Prokofiev would angrily chase away Maxim and Galya if they were merely being themselves within earshot of his room; but he himself was impervious to noise. All that bothered him was the barking of dogs: that insistent, hysterical sound cut right across the music he heard in his head. That was why he preferred cats to dogs. Cats were always happy to let him compose.

Those who did not know him, and who followed music only from a distance, probably imagined that the trauma of 1936 now lay well in the past. He had committed a great fault in writing *Lady Macbeth of Mtsensk*, and Power had properly castigated him. Repentant, he had composed a Soviet artist's creative reply to just criticism. Then, during the Great Patriotic War, he had written his Seventh Symphony, whose message of anti-Fascism had resounded across the world. And so, he had achieved forgiveness.

But those who understood how religion – and therefore Power – operated would have known better. The sinner might have been rehabilitated, but this did not mean that the sin itself had been expunged from the face of the earth; far from it. If the country's most famous composer could fall into error, how pernicious must that error be, and how dangerous to others. So the sin must be named, and reiterated, and its consequences eternally warned against. In other words, 'Muddle Instead of Music' had become a school text, and formed part of conservatoire courses in the history of music.

Nor could the chief sinner be allowed to continue on his way unshepherded. Those skilled in theolinguistics, who had studied the wording of that *Pravda* editorial as closely as it deserved, would have noticed an implicit reference to film music. Stalin had expressed a great appreciation of Dmitri Dmitrievich's soundtrack for the *Maxim* trilogy; while Zhdanov was known to play 'The Song of the Counterplan' to his wife on the piano every morning. It was the view of those at the highest level that Dmitri Dmitrievich Shostakovich was not a lost cause, and capable, *if properly directed*, of writing clear, realistic music. Art belonged to the People, as Lenin had decreed; and the cinema was of much greater use and value to the Soviet people than the opera. And so, Dmitri Dmitrievich now received proper direction, with the result that in 1940 he received the Red Banner of Labour as a specific reward for his film music. If he continued to tread the right path, this would surely prove the first of many such honours.

On the 5th of January 1948 – twelve years after his abbreviated visit to *Lady Macbeth of Mtsensk* – Stalin and his entourage were at the Bolshoi again, this time for Vano Muradeli's *The Great Friendship*. The composer, who was also chairman of the Soviet Music Fund, prided himself on writing music that was melodic, patriotic and socialist-realist. His opera, commissioned to celebrate the thirtieth anniversary of the October Revolution, and lavishly produced, had already enjoyed two months of great success. Its theme was the consolidation of Communist power in the Northern Caucasus during the Civil War.

Muradeli was a Georgian who knew his history; unfortunately for him, Stalin was also a Georgian, and knew his history better. Muradeli had portrayed the Georgians and Ossetians as rising up against the Red Army; whereas Stalin – not least because he had an Ossetian mother – knew that what actually happened in 1918–20 was that the Georgians and Ossetians had joined hands with the Russian Bolsheviks to fight in defence of the Revolution. It had been the Chechens and the Ingush whose counter-revolutionary actions had hindered the forging of the Great Friendship between the many peoples of the future Soviet Union.

Muradeli had compounded this politico-historical error with an equally gross musical one. He had included in his opera a lezghinka – which, as he doubtless knew, was Stalin's favourite dance. But instead of choosing an authentic and familiar lezghinka, thereby celebrating the folk traditions of the Caucasian people, the composer had egotistically chosen to invent his own dance 'in the style of the lezghinka'.

Five days later, Zhdanov had called a conference of seventy composers and musicologists to discuss the continuing and corrosive influence of formalism; and a month after this, the Central committee published its Official Decree 'On V. Muradeli's Opera *The Great Friendship*'. The composer learnt that his music, far from being as melodic and patriotic as he had supposed, quacked and grunted with the best of them. He too was pronounced a formalist, one serving up 'confused neuropathological combinations' and pandering to 'a narrow circle of experts and gourmets'. Needing to save his career, if not his skin, Muradeli came up with the best explanation he could: that he had been misled by others. He had been seduced and deceived into taking the wrong path, specifically by Dmitri Dmitrievich Shostakovich, and even more specifically by that composer's *Lady Macbeth of Mtsensk*.

Zhdanov reminded the nation's composers yet again that the criticisms embodied in the 1936 *Pravda* editorial were still valid: Music – harmonious, graceful music – was required, not Muddle. The chief culprits were named as Shostakovich, Prokofiev, Khachaturian, Myaskovsky and Shebalin. Their music was compared to a piercing road drill, and to the sound made by a 'musical gas chamber'. The word Zhdanov used was *dushegubka*, the name for the truck the Fascists used to drive around while inside their victims were being asphyxiated by its exhaust fumes.

Peace had returned, and so the world was upside down again; Terror had returned, and insanity with it. At a special congress called by the Union of Composers, a musicologist, whose offence had been to write a naively flattering book about Dmitri Dmitrievich, pleaded in desperate mitigation that at least he had never set foot in the composer's apartment. He called upon the composer Yuri Levitin to corroborate his statement. Levitin affirmed 'with a clear conscience' that the musicologist had never once breathed the contaminated air of the formalist's dwelling.

At the congress, his Eighth Symphony was targeted, as was Prokofiev's Sixth. Symphonies whose subject was war; symphonies which knew that war was tragic and terrible. But how little their formalist composers had understood: war was glorious and triumphant, and must be celebrated! Instead, they had indulged in 'unhealthy individualism' as well as 'pessimism'. He had declined to attend the congress. He was ill. In fact, he felt suicidal. He sent his excuses. His excuses were not accepted. Indeed, the congress would remain in session until such time as the great recidivist Dmitri Dmitrievich Shostakovich was able to attend: if necessary, they would send doctors to ascertain his medical condition and cure him. 'There is no escaping one's destiny' – and so he attended. He was instructed to make a public recantation. As he made his way to the platform, wondering what he might possibly say, a speech was thrust into his hand. He read it out tonelessly. He promised to follow Party directives in future and write melodic music for the People. In the middle of the official verbiage, he broke off from the text, lifted his head, looked around the hall, and said in a helpless voice, 'It always seems to me that when I write sincerely and as I truly feel, then my music cannot be "against" the People, and that, after all, I myself am a representative . . . in some small way . . . of the People.'

He had returned from the congress in a state of collapse. He was dismissed from his professorships at both the Moscow and Leningrad conservatoires. He wondered if it would be best to fall silent. Instead, to keep his sanity, he decided to write a series of preludes and fugues, after the example of Bach. Naturally, they were at first condemned: he was told that they sinned against 'surrounding reality'. Also, he could not forget the words – some his own, others provided for him – which had come out of his mouth in the past weeks. He had not just accepted the criticism of his work but applauded it. He had, in effect, repudiated *Lady Macbeth of Mtsensk*. He remembered what he had once said to a fellow composer about artistic honesty and personal honesty, and how much is allotted to each of us.

Then, after a year of disgrace, he had his Second Conversation with Power. 'The thunderclap comes from the heavens, not from a pile of dung,' as the poet has it. He was sitting at home with Nita and the composer Levitin on the 16th of March 1949 when the telephone rang. He answered it, listened, frowned, then said to the other two,

'Stalin is about to come on the line.'

Nita immediately ran into the next room and picked up the extension.

'Dmitri Dmitrievich,' the voice of Power began, 'how are you?'

'Thank you, Iosif Vissarionovich, everything is fine. Only, I am suffering somewhat from stomach ache.'

'I am sorry to hear that. We shall find a doctor for you.'

'No, thank you. I don't need anything. I have everything I need.'

'That is good.' There was a pause. Then the strong Georgian tones, the voice of a million radios and tannoys, asked if he was aware of the forthcoming Cultural and Scientific Congress for World Peace in New York. He said that he was.

'And what do you think of it?'

'I think, Iosif Vissarionovich, that peace is always better than war.'

'Good. So you are happy to attend as one of our representatives.'

'No, I cannot, I am afraid.'

'You *cannot*?'

'Comrade Molotov asked me. I told him I was not well enough to attend.'

'Then, as I say, we shall send a doctor to make you better.'

'It is not just that. I get air-sick. I cannot fly.'

'That will not be a problem. The doctor will prescribe you some pills.'

'That is kind of you.'

'So you will go?'

He paused. Part of him was conscious that the slightest wrong syllable might land him in a labour camp, while another part of him, to his surprise, was beyond fear.

'No, I really cannot go, Iosif Vissarionovich. For another reason.'

'Yes?'

'I do not have a tail-suit. I cannot perform in public without a tail-suit. And I am afraid I cannot afford one.'

'This is hardly my immediate business, Dmitri Dmitrievich, but I am sure that the workshop of the administration of the Central Committee will be able to make one that is to your satisfaction.'

'Thank you. But there is, I am afraid, another reason.'

'Which you are also about to tell me.'

Yes, it was just conceivably possible that Stalin did not know.

'The fact is, you see, that I am in a very difficult position. Over there, in America, my music is often played, whereas over here it is not played. They would ask me about it. So how am I to behave in such a situation?'

'What do you mean, Dmitri Dmitrievich, that your music is not played?'

'It is forbidden. As is the music of many of my colleagues in the Union of Composers.'

'Forbidden? Forbidden by whom?'

'By the State Commission for Repertoire. From the 14th of February last year. There is a long list of works which cannot be played. But the consequence, as you can imagine, Iosif Vissarionovich, is that concert managers are unwilling to programme any of my other compositions as well. And musicians are afraid to play them. So I am in effect blacklisted. As are my colleagues.'

'And who gave such an order?'

'It must have been one of the leading comrades.'

'No,' the voice of Power replied. 'We didn't give that order.'

He let Power consider the matter, which it did.

'No, we didn't give that order. It is a mistake. The mistake will be corrected. None of your works has been forbidden. They can all be freely played. This has always been the case. There will have to be an official reprimand.'

A few days later, along with other composers, he received a copy of the original banning order. Stapled to the top of it was a document recognising the decree as illegal, and reprimanding the State Commission for Repertoire for having issued it. The correction was signed, 'Chairman of the Council of Ministers of the USSR, I. Stalin.'

And so he had gone to New York.

To his mind, rudeness and tyranny were closely connected. It had not escaped his attention that Lenin, when dictating his political will and considering possible successors, judged Stalin's main fault to be 'rudeness'. And in his own world, he hated to see conductors described admiringly as 'dictators'. To be rude to an orchestral player who was doing his best was disgraceful. And these tyrants, these emperors of the baton, revelled in such terminology – as if an orchestra could only play well if whipped and derided and humiliated.

Toscanini was the worst. He had never seen the conductor in action; only knew him from records. But everything was wrong – tempi, spirit, nuance . . . Toscanini chopped up music like hash and then smeared a disgusting sauce all over it. This made him very angry. The 'maestro' had once sent him a recording of his Seventh Symphony. He had written back, pointing out the distinguished conductor's many errors. He did not know if Toscanini had received the letter or, if so, understood it. Perhaps he had assumed it must contain only praise, because soon afterwards the glorious news reached Moscow that he, Dmitri Dmitrievich Shostakovich, had been elected an honorary member of the Toscanini Society! And shortly after that, he began to receive gifts of gramophone records, all conducted by the great slave-driver. He never listened to them, of course, but piled them up as future presents. Not for friends, but for certain kinds of acquaintance, those he could tell in advance would be thrilled.

It was not just a matter of *amour propre*; or one that concerned only music. Such conductors screamed and cursed at orchestras, made scenes, threatened to sack the principal clarinet for coming in late. And the orchestra, compelled to put up with it, responded by telling stories behind the conductor's back – stories which made him out to be a 'real character'. Then they came to believe what this emperor of the baton himself believed: that they were only playing well because they were being whipped. They huddled together in a masochistic herd, occasionally dropping an ironic remark to one another, but essentially admiring their leader for his nobility and idealism, his sense of purpose, his ability to see more widely than those who just scraped and blew behind their desks. The maestro, harsh though he might of necessity be from time to time, was a great leader who must be followed. Now, who would still deny that an orchestra was a microcosm of society?

So when such a conductor, impatient of the mere score in front of him, imagined a mistake or a defect, he would always give the polite, ritual response he had long ago perfected.

And therefore he imagined the following conversation:

Power: 'Look, we have made the Revolution!'

Citizen Second Oboe: 'Yes, it's a wonderful revolution, of course. And a great improvement on what was there before. It really is a tremendous achievement. But I just wonder, from time to time . . . I might be completely wrong, of course, but was it absolutely necessary to shoot all those engineers, generals, scientists, musicologists? To send millions to the camps, to use slave labour and work it to death, to make everyone terrified, to extort false confessions in the name of the Revolution? To set up a system where, even at the edge of it, there are hundreds of men waiting each night to be dragged from their beds and taken to the Big House or the Lubyanka, to be tortured and made to sign their names to complete fabrications, then shot in the back of the head? I'm just wondering, you understand.'

Power: 'Yes, yes, I see your point. I'm sure you're right. But let's leave it for now. We'll make that change next time round.'

For some years, he had always made the same New Year's toast. For three hundred and sixty-four days of the year the country would have to listen to Power's insane daily insistence that all was for the best in the best possible of worlds, that Paradise had been created, or would be created quite soon when a few more logs had been chopped and a million more chips had flown, and a few hundred thousand more saboteurs had been shot. That happier times would come – unless they already had. And on the three hundred and sixty-fifth day, he would raise his glass, and say, in his most solemn voice: 'Let's drink to this – that things don't get any better!'

Of course, Russia had known tyrants before; that was why irony was so well developed here. 'Russia is the homeland of elephants,' as the saying went. Russia invented everything because . . . well, first because it was Russia, where delusions were normal; and second, because it was now Soviet Russia, the most socially advanced nation in history, where it was natural that things were discovered first. So when the Ford Motor Company abandoned its Ford Model A, the Soviet authorities bought the entire manufacturing plant: and behold, an authentic, Soviet-designed twenty-seater bus or light truck was upon the earth! The same with tractor factories: an American production line, imported from America, assembled by American experts, suddenly producing Soviet tractors. Or you copied a Leica camera and it was born afresh as a FED, named after Felix Dzerzhinsky, and thereby all the more Soviet. Who said the age of miracles was past? And all done with words, whose transformative powers were truly revolutionary. So, for instance, French bread. Everyone used to know it as such, and had been calling it such for years. Then one day, French bread disappeared from the shops. Instead, there was 'city bread' – exactly the same, of course, but now the patriotic product of a Soviet city.

★

When truth-speaking became impossible – because it led to immediate death – it had to be disguised. In Jewish folk music, despair is disguised as the dance. And so, truth's disguise was irony. Because the tyrant's ear is rarely tuned to hear it. The previous generation – those Old Bolsheviks who had made the Revolution – hadn't understood this, which was partly why so many of them perished. His generation had grasped it more instinctively. And so, the day after he had agreed to go to New York, he wrote the following letter:

> Dear Iosif Vissarionovich,
> First of all, please accept my heartfelt gratitude for the conversation that took place yesterday. You supported me very much, since the forthcoming trip to America had been worrying me greatly. I cannot but be proud of the confidence that has been placed in me; I will fulfil my duty. To speak on behalf of our great Soviet people in defence of peace is a great honour for me. My indisposition cannot serve as an impediment to the fulfilment of such a responsible mission.

As he signed it, he doubted the Great Leader and Helmsman would read it himself. Perhaps its contents would be conveyed to him, and then the letter would disappear into some file in some archive. It might stay there for decades, perhaps generations, perhaps 200,000,000,000 years; and then someone might read it, and wonder what exactly – if anything – he had meant by it.

In an ideal world, a young man should not be an ironical person. At that age, irony prevents growth, stunts the imagination. It is best to start life in a cheerful and open state of mind, believing in others, being optimistic, being frank with everyone about everything. And then, as one comes to understand things and people better, to develop a sense of irony. The natural progression of human life is from optimism to pessimism; and a sense of irony helps temper pessimism, helps produce balance, harmony.

But this was not an ideal world, and so irony grew in sudden and strange ways. Overnight, like a mushroom; disastrously, like a cancer.

Sarcasm was dangerous to its user, identifiable as the language of the wrecker and the saboteur. But irony – perhaps, sometimes, so he hoped – might enable you to preserve what you valued, even as the noise of time became loud enough to knock out window-panes. What did he value? Music, his family, love. Love, his family, music. The order of importance was liable to change. Could irony protect his music? In so far as music remained a secret language which allowed you to smuggle things past the wrong ears. But it could not exist only as a code: sometimes you ached to say things straightforwardly. Could irony protect his children? Maxim, at school, aged ten, had been obliged publicly to vilify his father in the course of a music exam. In such circumstances, what use was irony to Galya and Maxim?

As for love – not his own awkward, stumbling, blurting, annoying expressions of it, but love in general: he had always believed that love, as a force of nature, was indestructible; and that, when threatened, it could be protected, blanketed, swaddled in irony. Now he was less convinced. Tyranny had become so expert at destroying that why should it not destroy love as well, intentionally or not? Tyranny demanded that you love the Party, the State, the Great Leader and Helmsman, the People. But individual love – bourgeois and particularist – distracted from such grand, noble, meaningless, unthinking 'loves'. And in these times, people were always in danger of becoming less than fully themselves. If you terrorised them enough, they became something else, something diminished and reduced: mere techniques for survival. And so, it was not just an anxiety, but often a brute fear that he experienced: the fear that love's last days had come.

When you chop wood, the chips fly: that's what the builders of socialism liked to say. Yet what if you found, when you laid down your axe, that you had reduced the whole timberyard to nothing but chips?

In the middle of the war, he had set *Six Verses by British Poets* – one of the works banned by the State Commission for Repertoire, and then unbanned by Stalin. The fifth song was Shakespeare's Sonnet number 66: 'Tired with all these, for restful death I cry . . .' Like all Russians, he loved Shakespeare, and knew him well from Pasternak's translations. When Pasternak read Sonnet 66 in public, the audience would wait keenly through the first eight lines, eager for the ninth:

And art made tongue-tied by authority

At which point they would join in – some under their breath, some whisperingly, the boldest among them fortissimo, but all giving the lie to that line, all refusing to be tongue-tied.

Yes, he loved Shakespeare; before the war, he had written

the music for a stage production of *Hamlet*. Who could doubt that Shakespeare had a profound understanding of the human soul and the human condition? Was there a greater portrayal of the shattering of human illusions than *King Lear*? No, that was not quite right: not shattering, because that implied a single great crisis. Rather, what happened to human illusions was that they crumbled, they withered away. It was a long and wearisome process, like a toothache reaching far into the soul. But you can pull out a tooth and it will be gone. Illusions, however, even when dead, continue to rot and stink within us. We cannot escape their taste and smell. We carry them around with us all the time. He did.

How was it possible not to love Shakespeare? Shakespeare, after all, had loved music. His plays were full of it, even the tragedies. That moment when Lear awakes from madness to the sound of music . . . And that moment in *The Merchant of Venice* where Shakespeare says that the man who doesn't like music isn't trustworthy; that such a man would be capable of a base act, even murder or treason. So of course tyrants hated music, however strenuously they pretended to love it. Although they hated poetry more. He wished he had been at that reading by Leningrad poets when Akhmatova came on stage and the entire audience had risen instinctively to applaud her. A gesture which led Stalin to demand furiously: 'Who organised the standing up?' But, even more than poetry, tyrants hated and feared the theatre. Shakespeare held a mirror up to nature, and who could bear to see their own reflection? So *Hamlet* was banned for a long time; Stalin loathed the play almost as much as he loathed *Macbeth*.

And yet, for all this, for all that he was unparalleled in depicting tyrants knee-deep in blood, Shakespeare was a little naive. Because his monsters had doubts, bad dreams, pangs of conscience, guilt. They saw the spirits of those they had killed rising in front of them. But in real life, under real terror, what guilty conscience? What bad dreams? That was all sentimentality, false optimism, a hope that the world would be as we wanted it to be, rather than as it was. Those who chopped the wood and made the chips fly, those who smoked Belomory behind their desks at the Big House, those who signed the orders and made the telephone calls, closing a dossier and with it a life: how few of them had bad dreams, or ever saw the spirits of the dead rising to reproach them.

Ilf and Petrov had written: 'It is not enough to love Soviet power. It has to love you.' He himself would never be loved by Soviet power. He came from the wrong stock: the liberal intelligentsia of that suspect city St Leninsburg. Proletarian purity was as important to the Soviets as Aryan purity was to the Nazis. Further, he had the vanity, or foolishness, to notice and remember that what the Party had said yesterday was often in direct contradiction to what the Party was saying today. He wanted to be left alone with music and his family and his friends: the simplest of desires, yet one entirely unfulfillable. They wanted to engineer him along with everyone else. They wanted him to reforge himself, like a slave labourer on the White Sea Canal. They demanded 'an optimistic Shostakovich'. Even if the world was up to its neck in blood and farm slurry, you were expected to keep a smile on your face. But it was an artist's nature to be pessimistic and neurotic. So, they wanted you not to be an artist. But they already had so many artists who were not artists! As Chekhov put it, 'When they serve coffee, don't try to find beer in it.'

Also, he had none of the political skills required: he lacked the taste for licking rubber boots; he didn't know when to conspire against the innocent, when to betray friends. You needed someone like Khrennikov for that job. Tikhon Nikolayevich Khrennikov: a composer with the soul of a placeman. Khrennikov had an average ear for music, but perfect pitch when it came to power. They said he'd been hand-picked by Stalin, who had an instinct for such appointments. 'A fisherman sees another fisherman from afar,' as the saying goes.

Khrennikov came, appropriately enough, from a family of horse-traders. He thought it natural to take orders – as well as instructions in composition – from those with asses' ears. He had been attacking artists with more talent and originality than him since the mid-1930s, but when Stalin installed him as First Secretary of the Union of Composers in 1948, his power became official. He led the assault on formalists and rootless cosmopolitans, using all that terminology which made the ears bleed. Careers were ruined, work suppressed, families destroyed . . .

But you had to admire his understanding of power; at that, he was second to none. In shops, they used to display posters exhorting people how to behave: CUSTOMER AND CLERK, BE MUTUALLY POLITE. But the clerk was always more important than the customers: there were many of them and only one of him. Similarly, there were many composers but only one First Secretary. Towards his colleagues, Khrennikov behaved like a shop clerk who had never read the posters. He made his small power absolute: he denied them this, he rewarded them thus. And like any successful placeman, he never forgot where true power lay.

One of Dmitri Dmitrievich's former duties as professor at the Conservatoire had been to help examine the students on

Marxist–Leninist ideology. He would sit with the chief examiner beneath an enormous banner which declared: ART BELONGS TO THE PEOPLE – V. I. LENIN. As his own understanding of political theory was not profound, he remained largely silent, until one day his superior rebuked him for non-participation. So when the next student came in and the chief examiner nodded pointedly at his junior partner, he had asked her the simplest question he could think of.

'Tell me, whom does art belong to?'

The student looked completely baffled. Gently, he tried to help her along with a suggestion;

'Well, what did Lenin say?'

But she was too panicked to catch the clue, and for all his inclinations of the head and rolling upwards of the eyes, she failed to locate the answer.

In his view, she had done well, and when he occasionally noticed her in the corridors or stairways of the Conservatoire, he tried to give her an encouraging smile. Though given how she had failed to pick up the heaviest of hints, perhaps she thought his smiles, like his weird eye-rolling and head-jerking, were facial tics the distinguished composer was unable to control. Yet every time he passed her, the question reverberated in his head: 'Tell me, whom does art belong to?'

Art belongs to everybody and nobody. Art belongs to all time and no time. Art belongs to those who create it and those who savour it. Art no more belongs to the People and the Party than it once belonged to the aristocracy and the patron. Art is the whisper of history, heard above the noise of time. Art does not exist for art's sake: it exists for people's sake. But which people, and who defines them? He always thought of his own art as anti-aristocratic. Did he write, as his detractors maintained, for a bourgeois cosmopolitan elite? No. Did he write, as his detractors wanted him to, for the Donbass miner weary from his shift and in need of a soothing pick-me-up? No. He wrote music for everyone and no one. He wrote music for those who best appreciated the music he wrote, regardless of social origin. He wrote music for the ears that could hear. And he knew, therefore, that all true definitions of art are circular, and all untrue definitions of art ascribe to it a specific function.

A crane operator on a building site had once written a song and sent it to him. He had replied: 'Yours is such a wonderful profession. You are building houses which are needed so badly. My advice to you would be to keep going with your useful work.' He did so not because he believed a crane operator incapable of writing a song, but because this particular would-be composer showed as much talent as he himself would if put in the cabin of a crane and instructed to operate the levers. And he hoped that if, in the old days, an aristocrat had sent him a composition of similar worth, he would have had the fortitude to reply: 'Your Excellency, yours is such a distinguished and exacting position, being responsible on the one hand for maintaining the dignity of the aristocracy, and on the other for looking after the welfare of those who toil on your estates. My advice to you would be to keep going with your useful work.'

Stalin loved Beethoven. That's what Stalin said and what many musicians repeated. Stalin loved Beethoven because he was a true revolutionary, and because he was exalted, like the mountains. Stalin loved everything that was exalted, and that was why he loved Beethoven. It made his ears vomit when people told him this.

But there was a logical consequence to Stalin's love of Beethoven. The German had lived, of course, in bourgeois, capitalist times; so his solidarity with the proletariat, and his desire to see them throw off the yoke of servitude, inevitably sprang from a pre-Revolutionary political consciousness. He had been a forerunner. But now that the longed-for Revolution had taken place, now that the most politically advanced society on earth had been built, now that Utopia, the Garden of Eden and the Promised Land had all been rolled into one, it was obvious what must logically come forth: the Red Beethoven.

Wherever this ludicrous idea had come from – perhaps, like much else, it had sprung fully-formed from the Great Leader and Helmsman's own forehead – it was a concept which, once articulated, must find its own embodiment. Where was the Red Beethoven? And there took place a nationwide search unparalleled since Herod's quest for the infant Jesus. Well, if Russia was the homeland of elephants, why should it not also be the homeland of the Red Beethoven?

Stalin assured them that they were all screws in the mechanism of the State. But the Red Beethoven would be a mighty cog, hard to keep hidden. Self-evidently, he must be a pure proletarian and a member of the Party. Conditions which happily ruled out Dmitri Dmitrievich Shostakovich. They pointed instead, for a while, to Alexander Davidenko, who had been one of the leaders of the RAPM. His song 'They Wanted to Beat Us, to Beat Us', written to celebrate the glorious victory of the Red Army over the Chinese in 1929, had been even more popular than 'The Song of the

Counterplan'. Performed by soloists and massed choirs, by pianists, violinists and string quartets, it had stirred and cheered the land for a full decade. At one point, it seemed likely to replace all other available music.

Davidenko's credentials were impeccable. He had taught in a Moscow orphanage; he had supervised the lyrical activities of the Shoemakers' Union, the Union of Textile Workers, and even of the Black Sea Fleet at Sevastopol. He had written a genuine proletarian opera about the 1905 revolution. And yet, and yet . . . for all these qualifications, he remained stubbornly the composer of 'They Wanted to Beat Us, to Beat Us'. A properly melodic work, of course, and one utterly devoid of formalist tendencies. But somehow Davidenko had failed to build on that one great success and earn the title Stalin longed to bestow. Which could have been his good luck. The Red Beethoven, once crowned, might have ended up sharing the fate of the Red Napoleon. Or that of Boris Kornilov, lyricist of the *Counterplan*. All those much-loved words he put into 'The Song', and all those throats which had poured them out, couldn't save him from being arrested in 1937, and purged, as they liked to say, in 1938.

The search for the Red Beethoven might have been a comedy; except that nothing around Stalin was ever a comedy. The Great Leader and Helmsman could easily have decided that the Red Beethoven's failure to emerge had nothing to do with the organisation of musical life in the Soviet Union, and everything to do with the activities of wreckers and saboteurs. And who might want to sabotage the quest for the Red Beethoven? Why, formalist musicologists, of course! Give the NKVD enough time, and they would surely unearth the musicologists' plot. And that would be no joke either.

★

Ilf and Petrov had reported that there were no political offences in America, only criminal ones; and that Al Capone, while in his Alcatraz cell, had written anti-Soviet articles for the Hearst press. They also noted that Americans had 'primitive culinary skill and primitive rote voluptuousness'. He could not judge the latter characteristic, though there had been a strange incident with a woman during a concert interval. He had been in a roped-off area when he heard a female voice persistently calling his name. Assuming that she wanted to talk about his music, he had indicated that she should be let through. She stood in front of him, and said, with a bright, open friendliness,

'Hello. You resemble my cousin very much.'

It sounded like a line with which spies make contact, and so put him on the defensive. He asked if this cousin was Russian, by any chance.

'No,' she replied, 'he is one hundred per cent American. No, one hundred and ten per cent.'

He waited for her to mention his music – or that of the concert they were both attending – but she had delivered her message, and with another bright, open smile she left. He was puzzled. So he looked like someone else. Or someone else looked like him. Did this mean something, or did it mean nothing?

He knew, when he had agreed to attend the Cultural and Scientific Congress for World Peace, that he had no choice. He also suspected that he might be displayed as a figurehead, a representative of Soviet values. He had expected some Americans to be welcoming, others to be hostile. He had been instructed that after the congress he would travel outside New York, to peace rallies in Newark and Baltimore; he would also speak and play at Yale and Harvard. He was not surprised that some of these invitations had already been rescinded by the time they landed at LaGuardia; nor was he disappointed when the State Department sent them home early. All this was foreseeable. What he had not prepared himself for was that New York would turn out to be a place of the purest humiliation, and of moral shame.

The previous year, a young woman working at the Soviet consulate had jumped from a window and sought political asylum. So, during the congress, every day, a man paraded up and down outside the Waldorf Astoria with a placard reading SHOSTAKOVICH! JUMP THRU THE WINDOW! There had even been a proposal to construct nets around the building the Russian delegates were staying in, so that they could, if they wished, hurl themselves to freedom. By the end of the congress, he knew that the temptation was there – but that if he jumped, he would make sure that he missed any net.

No, that was not true; that was not being honest. He wouldn't aim for the pavement, for the simple reason that he wouldn't jump. How many times over the years had he made threats of suicide? Countless. And how many times had he actually tried? None. It wasn't that he didn't mean it. He felt, in the moment, genuinely suicidal, if it were possible to feel genuinely suicidal without passing to the act itself. Once or twice, he had even bought pills to do the job with, but never managed to keep this fact to himself – whereupon, after hours of tearful argument, the pills were confiscated. He had threatened his mother with suicide, and

Tanya, and then Nita. It was all perfectly genuine, just as it was all perfectly juvenile.

Tanya had laughed at his threats; his mother and Nita had taken them seriously. When he returned from the humiliation of the composers' congress, it was Nita who had dealt with him. But it was not just her moral strength that saved him; it was also the realisation on his part of exactly what he was doing. This time, he wasn't threatening Tanya or Nita or his mother with suicide; he was threatening Power. He was saying to the Union of Composers, to the cats who sharpened their claws on his soul, to Tikhon Nikolayevich Khrennikov, and to Stalin himself: Look what you have reduced me to, soon you will have my death on your hands and on your conscience. But he realised it was an empty threat, and Power's response hardly needed articulation. It would be this: Fine, go ahead, then we shall tell the world your story. The story of how you were up to your neck in the Tukhachevsky assassination plot, how for decades you schemed to undermine Soviet music, how you corrupted younger composers, sought to restore capitalism in the USSR, and were a leading element in the musicologists' plot which will soon be disclosed to the world. All of which is made plain in your suicide note. And that was why he could not kill himself: because then they would steal his story and rewrite it. He needed, if only in his own hopeless, hysterical way, to have some charge of his life, of his story.

The provoker of his moral shame was a man called Nabokov. Nicolas Nabokov. A composer himself in a small way. Who had left Russia in the Thirties and found a home in America. Machiavelli said that you should never trust an exile. This one was probably working for the CIA. As if any of that made it better.

At the first public meeting at the Waldorf Astoria, Nabokov sat in the front row, immediately opposite him, so close that their knees almost touched. With an insolent friendliness, this Russian with a well-cut American tweed jacket and brilliant-ined hair pointed out that the conference hall they were in was called the Perroquet Room. He explained that *Perroquet* meant *Parrot*. He translated the word into Russian. He smirked as if the irony would be apparent to all. The ease with which he had installed himself in the front row suggested that he was indeed in the pay of the American authorities. This had made Dmitri Dmitrievich even more nervous than he was already. When he tried to light a cigarette he would snap the match; or else, distracted, he would let his cigarette go out. Always, the tweed-clad exile was there with a lighter, clicking it smoothly under his nose, as if to say, Jump Thru The Window and you can have a nice shiny lighter like mine.

Anyone with an ounce of political understanding would know that he hadn't written the speeches he gave: the short one on the Friday and the very long one on the Saturday. He was handed them in advance and instructed to prepare his delivery. Naturally, he didn't. If they chose to rebuke him, he would point out that he was a composer, not a speech-maker. He read the Friday speech in a fast, uninflected gabble, reinforcing the fact that he was quite unfamiliar with the text. He carried straight on over punctuation marks as if they did not exist, pausing neither for effect nor reaction. This has absolutely nothing to do with me, his manner insisted. And while a translator read the English version, he ignored the gaze of

Mister Nicolas Nabokov, and did not light a cigarette for fear it would go out.

The next day's speech was different. He felt its length and weight in his hand, and so, without forewarning those concerned for his welfare, he merely read the first page and sat down, leaving the full text to the translator. As the English version was being read out, he followed the Russian original, curious to discover his own trite views on music and peace and the dangers to each of them. He began by attacking the enemies of peaceful coexistence and the aggressive activities of a group of militarists and hate-mongers who were intent on a third world war. He specifically accused the American government of building military bases thousands of miles from home, of provocatively trampling on its international obligations and treaties, and of perfecting new kinds of weapons of mass destruction. This act of wild discourtesy received a solid round of applause.

He then patronisingly explained to Americans how the Soviet music system was superior to any other on the face of the earth. This many orchestras, military bands, folk groups, choirs – proof of the active use of music in furthering the development of society. So, for instance, the peoples of Soviet Middle Asia and the Soviet Far East had in recent years thrown off the last remnants of the colonial status their cultures had been accorded under Tsarism. Uzbeks and Tajiks, together with other peoples of the far-flung Soviet Union, were benefitting from an unprecedented level and scope of musical development. At this juncture, he made a special point of assailing Mister Hanson Baldwin, military editor of the *New York Times*, for having written disparagingly of the populations of Soviet Asia in a recent article which naturally he had neither read nor heard of.

Such developments, he went on, inevitably led to a greater closeness and understanding between the People, the Party and the Soviet composer. If the composer must lead and inspire the People, then the People, through the Party, must also lead and inspire the composer. A spirit of active, constructive criticism existed, so that a composer might be warned if he was slipping into errors of petty subjectivity and introspective individualism, of formalism or cosmopolitanism; if – in short – he was losing touch with the People. He himself had not been without fault in this matter. He had departed from the true path of a Soviet composer, from big themes and contemporary images. He had lost contact with the masses and sought to please only a narrow stratum of sophisticated musicians. But the People could not remain indifferent to such straying, and so he had received public criticism which had directed him back to the proper road. It was a failure for which he had apologised and was now apologising again. He would seek to do better in the future.

So far, so banal – at least, he hoped it was to American ears. Another necessary confession of sins, even if at an exotic location. But then his eye skipped ahead and his mind froze. He saw in the text the name of the century's greatest composer, and an American accent marching towards it. First came a general condemnation of all musicians who believed in the doctrine of art for art's sake, rather than art for the sake of the masses; an attitude which had led to well-known perversions of music. The outstanding example of such perversion, he heard himself say, was the work of Igor Stravinsky, who had betrayed his native land and severed himself from his people by joining the clique of reactionary modern musicians. In exile, the composer had displayed moral barrenness, as was openly shown in his nihilistic writings, where he dismissed the masses as 'a quantitative term which has never entered my considerations', and openly boasted that 'My music does not express anything realistic.' He had thus confirmed the very meaninglessness and absence of content of his creations.

The supposed author of these words sat there motionless and unreacting, while inside he felt awash with shame and self-contempt. Why had he not seen this coming? He might have been able to change it, insert some modifications – if only into the Russian text as he read it out. He had foolishly imagined that his public indifference to his own speech would indicate a moral neutrality. That was as stupid as it was naive. He felt stunned, and could barely concentrate as his American voice turned its attention to Prokofiev. Sergei Sergeyevich had also recently strayed from the party line, and was in great danger of relapsing into formalism if he failed to heed the directives of the Central Committee. But whereas Stravinsky was a lost cause, Prokofiev might, if he were watchful, yet find great creative success by following the correct path.

He proceeded to a summing-up in which ardent hopes for world peace were combined with ignorant bigotry about music, for which he again received enormous applause. It was practically a Soviet ovation. There were some harmless questions from the floor, which he negotiated with the help of his translator and a friendly adviser who suddenly appeared beside his other ear. But then he saw a tweed-jacketed figure rise to his feet. This time not in the front row, but in a position from which the audience could see and hear the interrogation that now followed.

Mister Nicolas Nabokov began by explaining, with suave offensiveness, that he quite understood that the composer was here in an official capacity, and that the opinions expressed in his speech had been those of a delegate from Stalin's regime. But he wanted to pose some questions to him not as a delegate but rather as a composer – from one composer to another, as it were.

'Do you subscribe to the wholesale and bilious condemnation of Western music as daily expounded in the Soviet press and by the Soviet government?'

He felt the adviser's presence at his ear, but had no need of him. He knew what to answer because there was no choice. He had been led through the maze to the final room, the one containing no food as a reward, merely a trapdoor beneath his paws. And so, in a muttered monotone, he replied,

'Yes, I personally subscribe to those opinions.'

'Do you personally subscribe to the banning of Western music in Soviet concert halls?'

This allowed him a little more room for manoeuvre, and he replied,

'If music is good, it will be played.'

'Do you personally subscribe to the banning from Soviet concert halls of the works of Hindemith, Schoenberg and Stravinsky?'

Now he felt the sweat begin to drip behind his ears. As he took a little time with the translator, he thought briefly of the Marshal gripping his pen.

'Yes, I personally subscribe to such actions.'

'And do you personally subscribe to the views expressed in your speech today about the music of Stravinsky?'

'Yes, I personally subscribe to such views.'

'And do you personally subscribe to the views expressed about your music and that of other composers by Minister Zhdanov?'

Zhdanov, who had persecuted him since 1936, who had banned him and derided him and threatened him, who had compared his music to that of a road drill and a mobile gas chamber.

'Yes, I personally subscribe to the views expressed by Chairman Zhdanov.'

'Thank you,' said Nabokov, looking around the hall as if expecting applause. 'All is now perfectly clear.'

There was a story about Zhdanov much repeated in Moscow and Leningrad: the story of the music lesson. Gogol would have approved it; indeed, might even have written it. After the Central Committee's Decree of 1948, Zhdanov had instructed the country's leading composers to assemble at his ministry. In some versions, it was just himself and Prokofiev; in others, the whole slew of sinners and bandits. They were shown into a large room; on a platform stood a dais, and beside it a piano. There were no refreshments: no vodka to take the edge off one's fear, no sandwiches to quieten the stomach. They were kept waiting for some while. Then Zhdanov appeared with a pair of junior officials. He went to the dais and gazed down at the wreckers and sabo-teurs of Soviet music. He lectured them once again on their wickedness, delusion and vanity. He explained how, if they did not mend their ways, their game of clever ingenuity might end very badly. And then, just at the point where he had the composers shitting themselves, he produced a *coup de théâtre*. He went to the piano and gave them a masterclass. *This* – he thumped away discordantly, making the keys quack and grunt – was decadent, formalist music. And *this* – he played a soupy neo-romantic air, which in a film might accompany some previously haughty girl at last acknow-ledging her love – *this* was the graceful, realistic music of the kind the People craved and the Party demanded. He stood up, gave a mocking half-bow, and dismissed them with the back of his hand. The nation's composers had filed out, some promising to do better, others hanging their heads in shame.

It had never happened, of course. Zhdanov had lectured them until their ears bled, but was too clever to let his fat fingers desecrate the keyboard in that way. Even so, the story gained authority with each retelling, until some of those allegedly present had confirmed that, yes, it had happened exactly like that. And part of him wished that this conversation with Power, in which Power had arrogantly chosen its opponents' weapon, had really taken place. Nevertheless, it swiftly joined the songbook of believable myths circulating at this time. What mattered was not so much whether a particular story was factually true, but rather, what it signified. Though it was also the case that the more a story circulated, the truer it became.

He and Prokofiev had been attacked together, humiliated together, banned together and unbanned together. Yet in his opinion Sergei Sergeyevich never really understood what was going on. He was not a coward, either in his life or his music; but he saw it all – even Zhdanov's crazed and murderous attacks on the intelligentsia – as a personal problem to which there was, somewhere, a solution. Here was music, and here was his own particular talent; there lay Power, and bureaucracy, and politico-musicological theory. It was just a question of how the accommodation could be made so that he could go on being himself and writing his music. Or, to put it another way: Prokofiev completely failed to see the tragic dimension of what was happening.

★

One other good thing about the trip to New York: his tail-suit had been a success. It had fitted him very well.

He wondered, as the plane made its descent towards Reykjavik, if he should summon the stewardess and ask for a benzedrine inhaler. It could hardly make any difference now.

It was, he supposed, just possible that Nabokov, in some elaborate way, was being sympathetic to his plight, was trying to explain to the other delegates the true nature of this public masquerade. But if so, he was either a paid stooge or a political imbecile. In order to demonstrate the lack of individual freedom beneath the sun of Stalin's constitution, he was happy to sacrifice an individual life. Because that was what he was doing: If you don't want to Jump Thru The Window, why not put your head into this noose I've plaited for you? Why not tell the truth and die?

One of the pickets outside the Waldorf Astoria had carried a placard reading SHOSTAKOVICH – WE UNDERSTAND! How little they understood, even those like Nabokov who had lived some little time under Soviet power. And how smugly they would return to their cosy American apartments, happy to have put in a good day's work for virtue and liberty and world peace. They had no knowledge, and no imagination, these brave Western humanitarians. They came to Russia in eager little gangs, armed with vouchers for hotels and lunches and dinners, each one of them approved by the Soviet state, each keen to meet 'real Russians' and find out 'how they really felt' and 'what they really believed'. Which was the last thing they would be told, because you did not need to be paranoid to know that each group would contain an informant, and their guides would also be dutifully reporting back. One such gang had a meeting with Akhmatova and Zoshchenko. This was another of Stalin's tricks. You have heard that some of our artists are persecuted? Not at all, that is just your government's propaganda. You wanted to meet Akhmatova and Zoshchenko? Look, here they are – ask them whatever you wish.

And this group of Western humanitarians, already confirmed in their doe-eyed enthusiasm for Stalin, couldn't think of anything cleverer than to ask Akhmatova what she thought about Chairman Zhdanov's remarks and the Central Committee's resolution condemning her. Zhdanov had said that Akhmatova was poisoning the consciousness of Soviet youth with the rotten and putrid spirit of her poetry. Akhmatova got to her feet and replied that she considered both Chairman Zhdanov's speech and the Central Committee's resolution to be absolutely correct. And those concerned visitors had gone away clutching their meal vouchers and repeating to one another that the Western view of Soviet Russia was all a malign fantasy; that artists were not only well treated, but allowed to engage in constructive critical exchanges with even the highest echelons of Power. All of which proved how much more greatly the arts were valued in Russia than in their own decadent homelands.

But he was more revolted by the famous Western humanitarians who came to Russia and told its inhabitants they were living in paradise. Malraux, who praised the White Sea Canal without ever mentioning that its constructors were worked to death. Feuchtwanger, who fawned over Stalin and 'understood' how the show trials were a necessary part in the development of democracy. The singer Robeson, loud in his applause for political killing. Romain Rolland and Bernard Shaw, who disgusted him the more because they had the temerity to admire his music while ignoring how Power treated him and all other artists. He'd refused to meet Rolland, pretending to be ill. But Shaw was the worse of the two. Hunger in Russia? he had asked rhetorically. Nonsense, I've been fed as well as anywhere in the world. And it was he who said, 'You won't frighten me with the word "dictator".' And so the credulous fool hobnobbed with Stalin and saw nothing. Though why indeed should he be afraid of a dictator? They hadn't had one in England since the days of Cromwell. He had been forced to send Shaw the score of his Seventh Symphony. He should have added to his signature on its title page the number of peasants who had starved to death while the playwright was gorging himself in Moscow.

Then there were those who understood a little better, who supported you, and yet at the same time were disappointed in you. Who did not grasp the one simple fact about the Soviet Union: that it was impossible to tell the truth here and live. Who imagined they knew how Power operated and wanted you to fight it as they believed they would do in your position. In other words, they wanted your blood. They wanted martyrs to prove the regime's wickedness. But you were to be the martyr, not them. And how many martyrs would it take to prove that the regime was truly, monstrously, carnivorously evil? More, always more. They wanted the artist to be a gladiator, publicly fighting wild beasts, his blood staining the sand. That's what they required: in Pasternak's words, 'Total death, seriously.' Well, he would try to disappoint such idealists for as long as possible.

What they didn't understand, these self-nominated friends,

was how similar they were to Power itself: however much you gave, they wanted more.

Everyone had always wanted more from him than he was able to give. Yet all he had ever wanted to give them was music.

If only things were so simple.

In the imaginary conversations he sometimes had with these disappointed supporters, he would begin by explaining one small, basic fact of which they were almost certainly ignorant: that it was impossible in the Soviet Union to buy manuscript paper unless you were a member of the Union of Composers. Did they know that? Of course not. But Dmitri Dmitrievich, they would doubtless reply, if that is the case, surely you can buy blank paper, and with a ruler and pencil make your own? Surely you are not so easily put off practising your art?

Very well, he might reply, then let's start at the other end of things. If you are declared an enemy of the people, as he had once been, all those around you are tarnished and infected. Your family and friends, of course. But even a conductor who plays, or has played, or suggests playing, a work of yours; the members of a string quartet; the concert hall, be it ever so tiny, that stages your work; the very audience. How often, over the course of his career, had conductors and soloists suddenly become unavailable at the last minute? Sometimes from natural fear or understandable caution, sometimes after a hint from Power. Anyone, from Stalin down to Khrennikov, could stop his work being performed throughout the entire country for as long as they chose. They had already killed his career as a composer of opera. In his early years, many thought – and he had agreed with them – that this was where his best work would be done. But since they murdered *Lady Macbeth of Mtsensk*, he had not had an opera produced; nor finished any he had begun.

But surely, Dmitri Dmitrievich, you could write in the secrecy of your apartment; you could circulate your music; it could be played among friends; it could be smuggled out to the West like the manuscripts of poets and novelists? Yes, thank you, an excellent idea: new music of his, banned in Russia, played in the West. Could they imagine what a target that would make of him? It would be perfect proof that he was seeking to restore capitalism in the Soviet Union. But you could still write music? Yes, he could still write unperformed and unper-formable music. But music is intended to be heard in the period when it is written. Music is not like Chinese eggs: it does not improve by being kept underground for years and years.

But Dmitri Dmitrievich, you are being pessimistic. Music is immortal, music will always last and always be needed, music can say anything, music . . . and so on. He stopped his ears while they explained to him the nature of his own art. He applauded their idealism. And yes, music might be immortal, but composers alas are not. They are easily silenced, and even more easily killed. As for the accusation of pessimism – this was hardly the first time it had been voiced. And they would protest: No, no, you do not understand, we are just trying to help. So the next time they came, from their safe, rich lands, they would bring him vast batches of ready-printed manuscript paper.

In the war, on those slow, typhus-ridden trains between Kuibyshev and Moscow, he had worn amulets of garlic round his wrists and neck; they had helped him survive. But now he needed to wear them permanently: not against typhus, but against Power, against enemies, against hypocrites, and even against well-meaning friends.

He admired those who stood up and spoke truth to Power. He admired their bravery and their moral integrity. And sometimes he envied them; but it was complicated, because part of what he envied them was their death, their being put out of the agony of living. As he had stood waiting for the lift doors to open on the fifth floor of Bolshaya Pushkarskaya Street, terror was mixed with the pulsing desire to be taken away. He too had felt the vanity of transitory courage.

But these heroes, these martyrs, whose death often gave a double satisfaction – to the tyrant who ordered it, and to watching nations who wished to sympathise and yet feel superior – they did not die alone. Many around them would be destroyed as a result of their heroism. And therefore it was not simple, even when it was clear.

And of course, the intransigent logic ran in the opposite direction as well. If you saved yourself, you might also save those around you, those you loved. And since you would do anything in the world to save those you loved, you did anything in the world to save yourself. And because there was no choice, equally there was no possibility of avoiding moral corruption.

It had been a betrayal. He had betrayed Stravinsky, and in doing so, he had betrayed music. Later, he told Mravinsky that it had been the worst moment of his life.

★

When they reached Iceland, the plane had broken down, and they waited two days for a replacement. Then bad weather prevented them flying on to Frankfurt, so they diverted to Stockholm instead. Swedish musicians were delighted by the unscheduled descent of their distinguished colleague. Though when he was invited to name his favourite Swedish composers, he felt like a boy in short trousers – or like that girl student ignorant of whom art belonged to. He was about to cite Svendsen when he remembered that Svendsen was Norwegian. Still, the Swedes were too civilised to take offence, and the next morning he found in his hotel room a large parcel of records by local composers.

Not long after his return to Moscow, an article appeared under his name in the magazine *New World*. Interested to find out what he was supposed to think, he read of the congress's huge success, and of the State Department's furious decision to cut short the Soviet delegation's stay. 'On the way home I thought much about this,' he read of himself. 'Yes, the rulers of Washington fear our literature, our music, our speeches on peace – fear them because truth in any form hinders them from organising diversions against peace.'

'Life is not a walk across a field': it was also the last line of Pasternak's poem about Hamlet. And the previous line: 'I am alone; all round me drowns in falsehood.'

3: In the Car

All he knew was that this was the worst time of all.
The worst time was not the same as the most dangerous time.
Because the most dangerous time was not the time when you were most in danger.
This was something he hadn't understood before.

He sat in his chauffeured car while the landscape bumped and drifted past. He asked himself a question. It went like this:

> Lenin found music depressing.
> Stalin thought he understood and appreciated music.
> Khrushchev despised music.
> Which is the worst for a composer?

To some questions, there were no answers. Or at least, the questions stop when you die. Death cures the hunchback, as Khrushchev liked to say. He was not born one, but perhaps he had become one, morally, spiritually. A questioning hunchback. And perhaps death cures the questions as well as the questioner. And tragedies in hindsight look like farces.

When Lenin arrived at the Finland Station, Dmitri Dmitrievich and a group of schoolfellows had rushed there to greet the returning hero. It was a story he had told many times. However, since he had been a delicate, protected child, he might not have been allowed to go off just like that. It was more plausible that his Old Bolshevik uncle, Maxim Lavrentyevich Kostrikin, would have accompanied him to the station. He had told this version as well, many times. Both accounts helped burnish his revolutionary credentials. Ten-year-old Mitya at the Finland Station, inspired by the Great Leader! That image had not been a hindrance to his early career. But there was a third possibility: that he had not seen Lenin at all, and been nowhere near the station. He might just have adopted a schoolfellow's report of the event as his own. These days, he no longer knew which version to trust. Had he really, truly, been at the Finland Station? Well, he lies like an eyewitness, as the saying goes.

He lit another forbidden cigarette and stared at the chauffeur's ear. That, at least, was something solid and true: the chauffeur had an ear. And, no doubt, one on the other side, even though he couldn't see it. So it was an ear which existed only in his memory – or, more exactly, his imagination – until such time as he saw it again. Deliberately, he leant across until the wing and lobe of the other ear came into view. Another question solved, for the moment.

When he was little, his hero had been Nansen of the North. When he was grown up, the mere feel of snow beneath a pair of skis made him frightened, and his greatest act of exploration was to set off at Nita's request for the next village in search of cucumbers. Now that he was an old man, he was chauffeured around Moscow, usually by Irina, but sometimes by an official driver. He had become a Nansen of the Suburbs.

★

On his bedside table, always: a postcard of Titian's *The Tribute Money*.

Chekhov said that you should write everything – except denunciations.

Poor Anatoli Bashashkin. Denounced as Tito's stooge.

Akhmatova said that under Khrushchev, Power had become vegetarian. Maybe so; though you could just as easily kill someone by stuffing vegetables down their throat as by the traditional methods of the old meat-eating days.

He had returned from New York and composed *The Song of the Forests*, to an enormous, windy text by Dolmatovsky. Its theme was the regeneration of the steppes, and how Stalin, the Leader and Teacher, the Friend of Children, the Great Helmsman, the Great Father of the Nation, and the Great Railway Engineer, was now also the Great Gardener. 'Let us clothe the Motherland in forests!' – an injunction Dolmatovsky repeated ten or a dozen times. Under Stalin, the oratorio insisted, even apple trees grew more courageously, fighting off the frosts just as the Red Army had fought off the Nazis. The work's thunderous banality had ensured its immediate success. It helped him win his fourth Stalin Prize: 100,000 roubles, and a dacha. He had paid Caesar, and Caesar had not been ungrateful in return. In all, he had won the Stalin Prize six times. He also received the Order of Lenin at regular ten-year intervals: in 1946, 1956 and 1966. He swam in honours like a shrimp in shrimp-cocktail sauce. And he hoped to be dead by the time 1976 came around.

Perhaps courage was like beauty. A beautiful woman grows old: she sees only what has gone; others see only what remains. Some congratulated him on his endurance, his refusal to submit, the solid core beneath the hysterical surface. He saw only what was gone.

Stalin himself was long gone. The Great Gardener had gone to tend the grass in the Elysian Fields, and strengthen the morale of the apple trees there.

The red roses on Nita's grave, strewn all over. Every time he visited. And not sent by him.

Glikman had told him a story about Louis XIV. The Sun King had been as absolute a ruler as Stalin ever was. Yet he was always willing to give artists their proper due; to acknowledge their secret magic. One such was the poet Nicolas Boileau-Despréaux. And Louis XIV, in front of the entire court at Versailles, had announced, as if it were an everyday truth, 'Monsieur Despréaux has a better understanding of poetry than I do.' No doubt there was sycophantically disbelieving laughter from those who, in private and public, assured the great king that his understanding of poetry – and music, and painting, and architecture – was unmatched across the globe and down the centuries. And perhaps there was a tactical, diplomatic modesty about the remark in the first place. But still, it had been made.

Stalin, however, had so many advantages over that old king. His profound grasp of Marxist–Leninist theory, his intuitive understanding of the People, his love of folk music, his ability to sniff out formalist plots . . . Oh, enough, enough. He would make his own ears bleed.

But even the Great Gardener in his guise as the Great Musicologist had been unable to sniff out the location of the Red Beethoven. Davidenko had disappointed – not least by dying in his mid-thirties. And the Red Beethoven never did turn up.

He liked to tell the story of Tinyakov. A handsome man, a good poet. He lived in Petersburg and wrote about love and flowers and other lofty subjects. Then the Revolution came, and soon he was Tinyakov the poet of Leningrad, who wrote not about love and flowers, but about how hungry he was. And after a while things got so bad that he would stand on a street corner with a placard round his neck reading POET. And since Russians valued their poets, passers-by used to give him money. Tinyakov liked to claim that he had earned far more money from begging than he ever did from his verses, and so was able each evening to wind up in a fancy restaurant.

Was that last detail true? He wondered. But poets were allowed exaggeration. As for himself, he did not need a placard – he had three Orders of Lenin and six Stalin Prizes round his neck and ate in the restaurant of the Union of Composers.

★

One man, sly and swarthy, with a dangling ruby earring, grips a coin between thumb and forefinger. He shows it to a second, paler man, who does not touch it, but instead looks the first man straight in the eye.

There had been that strange time when Power, having decided that Dmitri Dmitrievich Shostakovich was a salvageable case, had tried a new tactic with him. Instead of waiting for the end result – a finished composition which would then have to be examined by politico-musicological experts before being approved or condemned – the Party, in its wisdom, decided instead to begin at the beginning: with the state of his ideological soul. Thoughtfully, generously, the Union of Composers appointed a tutor, Comrade Troshin, a grave and elderly sociologist, to help him understand the principles of Marxism–Leninism – to help him reforge himself. He was sent a reading list, which consisted entirely of works by Comrade Stalin, such as *Marxism and Questions of Linguistics*, and *Economic Problems of Socialism in the USSR*. Troshin then came to the apartment and explained his function. He was there because, alas, even distinguished composers were capable of serious error, as had been publicly aired in recent years. To avoid repetition of such errors, Dmitri Dmitrievich's level of political, economic and ideological understanding must be raised. The composer received his uninvited guest's statement of intent with due seriousness, while expressing his regret that work on a new symphony dedicated to the memory of Lenin had so far prevented him from reading all of the library which had been so kindly delivered.

Comrade Troshin looked round the composer's study. He was neither a devious nor a threatening man, just one of those diligent, unquestioning functionaries that every regime throws up.

'And this is where you work.'

'Indeed.'

The tutor stood up, made a step or two in each direction, and praised the room's general arrangement. Then, with an apologetic smile, he observed:

'But there is one thing missing in the study of a distinguished Soviet composer.'

The distinguished Soviet composer in turn stood up, looked around the walls and bookcases he knew so well, and shook his head with equal apology, as if embarrassed to be failing at his tutor's first question.

'There is no portrait on your walls of Comrade Stalin.'

A daunting silence ensued. The composer lit a cigarette and paced the room, as if searching for the cause of this hideous solecism, or as if he might find the necessary icon beneath this cushion, that rug. Finally, he assured Troshin that he would take immediate steps to procure the best available picture of the Great Leader.

'Well, that's fine, then,' replied Troshin. 'Now let's get down to business.'

He was required, from time to time, to make a précis of Stalin's turgid wisdom. Happily, Glikman offered to do the job for him, and the composer's patriotic insights into the Great Gardener's oeuvre were posted to him on a regular basis from Leningrad. After a while, other key texts were added to the curriculum: for instance, G. M. Malenkov's 'The Characteristics of Creativity in Art', a reprint of his speech to the 19th Party Congress.

Troshin's presence in his life, earnest and persistent, was received on his part with polite evasiveness and secret mockery.

They played their roles as instructor and pupil with straight faces; no doubt, Troshin did not have another face to offer. He believed all too evidently in the virtuous purpose of his task, and the composer treated him civilly, recognising that these unwanted visits amounted to a kind of protection. And yet each of them was aware that their charade might have serious consequences.

In that time, there were two phrases – one a question and one a statement – which would cause the sweat to pour and strong men to shit their pants. The question was: 'Does Stalin know?' The statement, even more alarming, was: 'Stalin knows.' And since Stalin was accorded supernatural powers – he never made a mistake, he commanded everything and was everywhere – the mere terrestrial beings under his power felt, or imagined, his eye being constantly on them. So what if Comrade Troshin failed to teach the precepts of Karlo-Marlo and their descendants in a satisfactory way? What if his pupil, outwardly solemn but inwardly whimsical, failed to learn? What then for the Troshins of this world? They both knew the answer. If the tutor offered protection to his pupil, the pupil had a certain responsibility towards his tutor.

But there was a third phrase, whispered about him as it had been whispered about others – Pasternak, for example: 'Stalin says he is not to be touched.' Sometimes this statement was a fact, sometimes a wild theory or envious supposition. Why had he survived being a protégé of the traitor Tukhachevsky? Why had he survived those words, 'It is a game of clever ingenuity that may end very badly'? Why had he survived being named an enemy of the people by the newspapers? Why had Zakrevsky disappeared between a Saturday and a Monday?

Why had he been spared when so many around him had been arrested, exiled, murdered, or had disappeared into a fate which might become clear only decades later? One answer would fit all those questions: 'Stalin says he is not to be touched.'

If so – and he had no way of knowing, any more than those who uttered the phrase – he would be a fool to imagine that it afforded him permanent protection. Just to be noticed by Stalin was much more dangerous than an existence of anonymous obscurity. Those in favour rarely stayed in favour; it was just a question of when they fell. How many important cogs in the machinery of Soviet life had subsequently turned out, after some imperceptible shift of the light, to have been hindering the other cogs all along?

The car slowed at an intersection, and then he heard the clatter of a ratchet as the chauffeur pulled on the handbrake. He remembered buying their first Pobeda. At the time, regulations insisted that the purchaser be present when the car was handed over. He still held a licence from before the war, so went to the garage by himself and took delivery of the car. Driving home, he wasn't very impressed by the Pobeda's performance, and wondered if he'd been sold a dud. He parked, and was fiddling with the lock when a passer-by called out, 'Hey, you with the specs, what's wrong with your car?' The wheels were disgorging smoke: he had driven all the way from the garage with the handbrake on. Cars didn't seem to like him – that was the truth.

He remembered another girl he had examined in his guise as Professor of Bolshevik Ideology at the Conservatoire. The chief examiner had left the room for a while, and he found himself in sole charge. The student was so nervous, twisting in her hand the page of questions she was expected to answer, that he had taken pity on her.

'Well,' he said, 'let's put all those official questions to one side. Instead, I'll ask you this: what is Revisionism?'

It was a question even he could have answered. Revisionism was so loathsome and heretical a concept that the word itself practically had horns growing out of its head.

The girl reflected for a while, and then answered confidently, 'Revisionism is the highest stage in the development of Marxism–Leninism.'

Whereupon he had smiled, and given her the best mark possible.

When all else failed, when there seemed to be nothing but nonsense in the world, he held to this: that good music would always be good music, and great music was impregnable. You could play Bach's preludes and fugues at any tempo, with any dynamics, and they would still be great music, proof even against the wretch who brought ten thumbs to the keyboard. And in the same way, you could not play such music cynically.

In 1949, when the attacks on him were still continuing, he had written his fourth string quartet. The Borodins had learnt it, and played it for the Ministry of Culture's Directorate of Musical Institutions, which needed to approve any new work before it could be performed – and before the composer could be paid. Given his precarious status, he was not sanguine; but to everyone's surprise the audition was a success, the piece authorised and money forthcoming. Soon afterwards, the story began to circulate that the Borodins had learnt to play the quartet in two different ways: authentically and strategically. The first was the way the composer had intended; whereas in the second, designed to get past musical officialdom, the players emphasised the 'optimistic' aspects of the piece, and its accordance with the norms of socialist art. This was held to be a perfect example of the use of irony as a defence against Power.

It had never happened, of course, but the story was repeated often enough for its veracity to be accepted. This was a nonsense: it wasn't true – it couldn't be true – because you cannot lie in music. The Borodins could only play the fourth quartet in the way the composer intended. Music – good music, great music – had a hard, irreducible purity to it. It might be bitter and despairing and pessimistic, but it could never be cynical. If music is tragic, those with asses' ears accuse it of being cynical. But when a composer is bitter, or in despair, or pessimistic, that still means he believes in something.

What could be put up against the noise of time? Only that music which is inside ourselves – the music of our being – which is transformed by some into real music. Which, over the decades, if it is strong and true and pure enough to drown out the noise of time, is transformed into the whisper of history.

This was what he held to.

His civil, tedious and fraudulent conversations with Comrade Troshin continued. One afternoon, the tutor's mood was uncharacteristically animated.

'Is it true,' he asked, 'is it true – I've just recently been told – that a few years ago Iosif Vissarionovich rang you up in person?'

'Yes, it is true.'

The composer pointed at the telephone on the wall, even though it was not the one he had used. Troshin gazed at the instrument as if it ought already to be in a museum.

'What a truly great man Stalin is! With all the cares of state, with all that he has to deal with, he knows even about some Shostakovich. He rules half the world and yet he has time for you!'

'Yes, yes,' he agreed with feigned zeal. 'It is truly amazing.'

'I am aware that you are a well-known composer,' the tutor continued, 'but who are you in comparison with our Great Leader?'

Guessing that Troshin would not be familiar with the text of the Dargomyzhsky romance, he replied gravely, 'I am a worm in comparison with His Excellency. I am a worm.'

'Yes, that's just it, you are a worm indeed. And it's a good thing that you now appear to possess a healthy sense of self-criticism.'

As if eager for more such praise, he had repeated, as soberly as he could manage, 'Yes, I'm a worm, a mere worm.'

Troshin went away well pleased with the progress that had been made.

But the composer's study never did display the finest portrait of Stalin that Moscow could sell. Only a few months into Dmitri Dmitrievich's re-education, the objective circumstances of Soviet reality changed. In other words, Stalin died. And the tutor's visits came to an end.

★

As the chauffeur braked, the car pulled to the left. It was a Volga, comfortable enough. He had always wanted to own a foreign car. He had always wanted, very specifically, a Mercedes. He had foreign currency sitting in the copyright bureau, but was never allowed to spend it on a foreign car. What is wrong with our Soviet cars, Dmitri Dmitrievich? Do they not take you from place to place, are they not reliable, and built with Soviet roads in mind? How would it look if our most distinguished composer was seen to insult the Soviet motor industry by buying a Mercedes? Do members of the Politburo drive around in capitalist vehicles? Surely you can see that it is quite impossible.

Prokofiev had been allowed to import a new Ford from the West. Sergei Sergeyevich was very pleased with it, until the day it proved too difficult for him to manage, and in the middle of Moscow he ran over a young woman. Somehow, that was typical of Prokofiev. He always came at the world from the wrong direction.

Of course, no one dies at exactly the correct moment: some too early, some too late. A few get the year more or less right, but then choose completely the wrong date. Poor Prokofiev – to die on exactly the same day as Stalin! Sergei Sergeyevich suffered a stroke at eight in the evening and died at nine. Stalin died fifty minutes later. To die not even knowing that the Great Tyrant had expired! Well, that was Sergei Sergeyevich for you. Despite being a punctilious timekeeper, he was always half out of step with Russia. So his dying had shown a foolish synchronicity.

The names of Prokofiev and Shostakovich would always be linked. But though manacled together, they were never friends. They – mostly – admired one another's music, but the West had penetrated too deeply into Sergei Sergeyevich. He had left Russia in 1918, and, apart from brief returns – as with a pair of puzzling pyjamas – had stayed away until 1936. By then he had lost touch with Soviet reality. He imagined that he would be applauded for his patriotic homecoming, that tyranny would be grateful – how naive was that? And when they were arraigned together before tribunals of musical bureaucrats, Sergei Sergeyevich thought only of musical solutions. They had asked him what was wrong with his colleague Dmitri Dmitrievich's Eighth Symphony. Nothing that couldn't be fixed, he replied, ever the pragmatist: it just needs a clearer melodic line, and the second and fourth movements should be cut. And when faced with criticism of his own work, his response was: look, I have a multiplicity of styles, just tell me which you would prefer me to use. He was proud of his facility – but that was not what was being asked of him. They didn't want you to fake adherence to their banal taste and meaningless critical slogans – they wanted you actually to believe in them. They wanted your complicity, your compliance, your corruption. And Sergei Sergeyevich had never really understood this. He said – and it was brave of him to do so – that when a piece was killingly denounced for 'formalism', it was 'a simple matter of not understanding something on first hearing'. He had a strange kind of sophisticated innocence. But really, the man had the soul of a goose.

He often thought of Sergei Sergeyevich in wartime exile, selling off his finely-cut European suits in the market at Alma-Ata. They said he was a skilful trader and always got the best price. Whose shoulders would those suits be on now? But it wasn't just his clothes: Prokofiev enjoyed all the trappings of success. And he understood fame in a Western way. He liked to say things were 'amusing'. Despite his public praise of *Lady Macbeth of Mtsensk*, when he leafed through the score in its composer's presence, he had pronounced the work 'amusing'. It was a word which should have been banned until the day after Stalin's death. Which Sergei Sergeyevich had not lived to see.

He himself had never been tempted by a life abroad. He was a Russian composer who lived in Russia. He declined to imagine any alternative. Though he had experienced his own brief moment of Western fame. In New York, he had gone to a pharmacy for some aspirin. Ten minutes after he left, an assistant was seen fixing a sign in the window. It read: DMITRI SHOSTAKOVICH SHOPS HERE.

He no longer expected to be killed – that fear was long in the past. But being killed had never been the worst. In January 1948 his old friend Solomon Mikhoels, director of the Moscow Jewish Theatre, was murdered on Stalin's orders. The day the news came out, he had spent five hours being hectored by Zhdanov for distorting Soviet reality, failing to celebrate the nation's glorious victories, and eating out of the hands of its enemies. Afterwards, he went straight to Mikhoels's apartment. He had embraced his friend's daughter and her husband. Then, standing with his back to the crowd of silent, fearful mourners, with his face almost pushing into the bookcase, he said to them, in a quiet, clear voice, 'I envy him.' He meant it: death was preferable to endless terror.

★

But endless terror continued for another five years. Until Stalin died, and Nikita Khrushchev emerged. There was the promise of a thaw, cautious hope, incautious elation. And yes, things did get easier, and some filthy secrets emerged; but there was no sudden idealistic attachment to the truth, merely an awareness that it could now be used to political advantage. And Power itself did not diminish; it just mutated. The terrified wait by the lift and the bullet to the back of the head became things of the past. But Power did not lose interest in him; hands still reached out – and since childhood he had always held a fear of grabbing hands.

Nikita the Corncob. Who would go into tirades about 'abstractionists and pederasts' – they being obviously the same thing. Just as Zhdanov had once denounced Akhmatova as 'both a slut and a nun'. Nikita the Corncob, at a meeting of writers and artists, had said of Dmitri Dmitrievich, 'Oh, his music's nothing but jazz – it gives you the bellyache. And I'm to clap my hands? But with jazz – you get colic.' However, this was better than being told you ate out of the hands of the nation's enemies. And in these more liberal times, some of those gathered to meet the First Secretary were allowed, if with proper deference, to offer a contrary opinion. There had even been a poet bold – or crazy – enough to maintain that there were great artists among the abstractionists. He had mentioned the name of Picasso. To which the Corncob had replied brusquely,

'Death cures the hunchback.'

In the old days, such an exchange might have led to the insolent poet being reminded that he was playing a dangerous game which might end very badly. But this was Khrushchev. His rantings made the lackeys with brass faces sway in one direction, then another; but you did not immediately fear for your future. One day the Corncob might announce that your music gave him the bellyache, and the next, after a fancy banquet at the Union of Composers' Congress, he might actually praise you. That evening he had been holding forth about how, if music were half decent, he could just about listen to it on the radio – except when they transmitted stuff which sounded, well, like the cawing of rooks . . . And as the lackeys with brass faces were laughing away, his eye fell on the well-known composer of bellyaching jazz. But the First Secretary was in a benign, indeed forgiving, mood.

'Now, there's Dmitri Dmitrievich – he saw the light at the very beginning of the war with his . . . what d'you call it, ah, his symphony.'

Suddenly, he was not in disfavour, and Lyudmila Lyadova, concocter of popular songs, came over and kissed him, then witlessly announced how everyone loved him. Well, it really did not matter either way, because things were no longer as they had once been.

But this was where he made his mistake. Before, there was death; now, there was life. Before, men shat in their pants; now, they were allowed to disagree. Before, there were orders; now, there were suggestions. So his Conversations with Power became, without him at first recognising it, more dangerous to the soul. Before, they had tested the extent of his courage; now, they tested the extent of his cowardice. And they worked with diligence and know-how, with an intense but essentially disinterested professionalism, like priests working for the soul of a dying man.

★

He himself knew little about visual art, and could hardly argue with that poet about abstractionism; but he knew Picasso for a bastard and a coward. How easy it was to be a Communist when you weren't living under Communism! Picasso had spent a lifetime painting his shit and hailing Soviet power. Yet God forbid that any poor little artist suffering under Soviet power should try to paint like Picasso. He was free to speak the truth – why didn't he do so on behalf of those who couldn't? Instead, he sat like a rich man in Paris and the south of France painting his revolting dove of peace time and time again. He loathed the sight of that bloody dove. And he loathed the slavery of ideas as much as he loathed physical slavery.

Or Jean-Paul Sartre. He'd once taken Maxim to the copyright bureau next to the Tretyakov Gallery, and there, standing at the cashier's desk, was the great philosopher, counting out his fat wad of roubles with great care. In those days royalties were paid out to foreign writers only in exceptional cases. In a whisper, he had explained those circumstances to Maxim: 'We don't deny material incentives if a person leaves the camp of reaction for the camp of progress.'

Stravinsky was a different matter. His love and reverence for Stravinsky's music had never wavered. And as proof, he kept a large photograph of his fellow composer beneath the glass of his desktop. He looked at it every day and remembered that gilded salon at the Waldorf Astoria; remembered the betrayal, and his moral shame.

When the Thaw came, Stravinsky's music was played again, and Khrushchev, who knew as much about music as a pig knows about oranges, was persuaded to invite the famous exile to return for a visit. It would be a great propaganda coup, apart from anything else. Perhaps they hoped in some way to turn Stravinsky back from a cosmopolitan into a purely Russian composer. And perhaps Stravinsky for his part hoped to rediscover some remnants of the old Russia he had long ago left behind. If so, both dreams were disappointed. But Stravinsky had some fun. For decades he had been denounced by the Soviet authorities as a lackey of capitalism. So when some musical bureaucrat came towards him with a fake smile and an extended hand, Stravinsky, instead of offering his own hand, gave the official the head of his walking stick to shake. The gesture was clear: who's the lackey now?

But it was one thing to humiliate a Soviet bureaucrat once Power had grown vegetarian; another to protest when Power was carnivorous. And Stravinsky had spent decades sitting on top of his American Mount Olympus, aloof, egocentric, unconcerned when artists and writers and their families were being hunted down in his native land; were imprisoned, exiled, murdered. Did he utter a single public word of protest while breathing the air of freedom? That silence had been contemptible; and just as he revered Stravinsky the composer, so he despised Stravinsky the thinker. Well, perhaps that answered his question about personal honesty and artistic honesty; lack of the former didn't necessarily contaminate the latter.

They had met twice during the course of the exile's visit. Neither occasion had been a success. He himself was as apprehensive and self-conscious as Stravinsky was bold and self-assured. What could they possibly have to say to one another? So he had asked,

'What do you think of Puccini?'

'I loathe him,' Stravinsky had replied.

To which he had answered, 'So do I.'

Did either of them mean it – mean it as absolutely as they had spoken? Probably not. One was being instinctively dominant, the other instinctively submissive. That was the trouble with 'historic meetings'.

He had also had a 'historic meeting' with Akhmatova. He had invited her to visit him at Repino. She came. He sat in silence; so did she; after twenty such minutes, she rose and left. She said afterwards, 'It was wonderful.'

There was much to be said for silence, that place where words run out and music begins; also, where music runs out. He sometimes compared his situation with that of Sibelius, who wrote nothing in the last third of his life, instead merely sat there embodying the Glory of the Finnish People. This was not a bad way to exist; but he doubted he had the strength for silence.

Sibelius had apparently been full of dissatisfaction and self-contempt. It was said that the day he burnt all his surviving manuscripts he felt a weight lifted from his shoulders. That made sense. As did the connection between self-contempt and alcohol, the one inciting the other. He knew that connection, that incitement all too well.

There was a different version of Akhmatova's visit to Repino going the rounds. In this, her report went: 'We talked for twenty minutes. It was wonderful.' If she'd actually said that, she was fantasising. But that was the trouble with 'historic meetings'. What was posterity to believe? Sometimes, he thought that there was a different version of everything.

When he and Stravinsky had discussed conducting, he had confessed: 'I do not know how not to be afraid.' At the time, he thought he was only talking about conducting. Now, he was not so sure.

He was no longer afraid of being killed – that was true, and should have been an advantage. He knew he would be allowed to live, and receive the best medical attention. But, in a way, that was worse. Because it is always possible to bring the living to a lower point. You cannot say that of the dead.

He had gone to Helsinki to receive the Sibelius Prize. In the same year, simply between the months of May and October, he had been made a member of the Accademia di Santa Cecilia in Rome, a Commandeur de l'Ordre des Arts et des Lettres in Paris, an honorary doctor of Oxford University, and a member of the Royal Academy of Music in London. He swam in honours like a shrimp in shrimp-cocktail sauce. In Oxford, he met Poulenc, who was also receiving an honorary degree. They were shown a piano which had apparently once belonged to Fauré. Respectfully, each had played a few chords.

Such occasions would have given a normal man great pleasure, and be received as the sweet and merited consolations of age. But he was not a normal man; and as they showered him with honours, they also stuffed him with vegetables. How cunningly different their attacks on him now were. They came with a smile, and several glasses of vodka, and sympathetic jokes about giving the First Secretary bellyache, and then the

flattery, and the wheedling, and the silences and the expectations . . . and sometimes he was drunk, and sometimes he
hadn't really known what was happening until he got home,
or went to the apartment of a friend, where he might collapse
in tears and sobs and cries of self-loathing. It had got to the
point where he despised being the person he was, on an almost
daily basis. He should have died years ago.

Also, they had killed *Lady Macbeth of Mtsensk* a second time.
It had been banned for twenty years, since the day Molotov,
Mikoyan and Zhdanov had chortled and sneered away while
Stalin skulked behind a curtain. With Stalin and Zhdanov dead,
and the Thaw declared, he had revised the opera with the
help of Glikman, his friend and helpmeet since the early
Thirties. Glikman, who had sat beside him the day he pasted
'Muddle Instead of Music' into his scrapbook. Their new
version went to the Leningrad Maly Theatre, who applied for
permission to stage it. But the process stalled, and he was
advised that the best hope of accelerating it was for the
composer himself to write a letter petitioning the First Deputy
Chairman of the Council of Ministers of the USSR. Which
was of course humiliating, because the First Deputy Chairman
of the Council of Ministers of the USSR was none other
than Vyacheslav Mikhailovich Molotov.

Still, he wrote the letter, and the Ministry of Culture
appointed a committee to examine this new version. As a
gesture of respect to the nation's most distinguished composer,
the committee would come to his apartment on the
Mozhaiskoye Highway. Glikman was there, as were the
director of the Maly Theatre and its orchestra's conductor.
The committee itself consisted of the composers Kabalevsky

and Chulaki, the musicologist Khubov and the conductor Tselikovsky. He had been very nervous before their arrival. He handed them typed copies of the libretto. Then he played through the entire opera, singing all the parts, while Maxim sat at his elbow and turned the score.

There had been a pause, which extended into an awkward silence, and then the committee began its work. Twenty years had passed, and they were not four men of power sitting in a bulletproof box; instead, they were four men of music – sophisticated men with no blood on their hands – sitting in the apartment of a fellow musician. And yet it was as if nothing had changed. They compared what they had heard with what had been written two decades previously, and found it just as wanting. They argued that since 'Muddle Instead of Music' had never been officially withdrawn, its tenets were still applicable. One of them being that his music hooted and quacked and grunted and gasped for breath. Glikman had tried to argue but was shouted down by Khubov. Kabalevsky praised certain sections of the work while asserting that as a whole it was morally reprehensible because it justified the actions of a murderess and whore. The two from the Maly Theatre were silent; he himself sat on the sofa with his eyes closed, listening to the committee members seek to outdo one another in abuse.

They voted unanimously not to recommend the opera's revival because of its glaring artistic and ideological faults. Kabalevsky, seeking to ingratiate, had said to him,

'Mitya, why the hurry? The time for your opera has not yet come.'

Nor, it seemed to him, would it ever now come. He had thanked the committee for their 'critique', and then gone with Glikman to the private room of the Aragvi restaurant, where they had got very drunk. That was one of the few advantages he found in age: he no longer collapsed after a couple of glasses. He could go on getting drunk all night if he so wished.

Diaghilev was always trying to persuade Rimsky-Korsakov to come to Paris. The composer kept on refusing. Eventually, the lordly impresario came up with a stratagem which effectively compelled the composer's presence. A resigned Korsakov sent a postcard which read: 'If we're going, then let's go, as the parrot said to the cat which was dragging it downstairs by the tail.'

Yes, that was what his life had often felt like. And his head had been bumped on far too many steps.

He had always been a meticulous man. He visited the barber every two months and the dentist just as often – being as anxious as he was meticulous. He was always washing his hands; he emptied ashtrays as soon as he saw two stubs in them. He liked to know that things were working properly: water, electricity, plumbing. His calendar was marked with the birthdays of family, friends and colleagues, and there would always be a card or a telegram for those on the list. When visiting his dacha outside Moscow, his first action was always to send himself a postcard to check the reliability of the mail. If this at times became a slight mania, it was a necessary one. If the wider world becomes uncontrollable, you must make sure to control what areas you can. However tiny they might be.

★

His body was just as nervous as it always had been; perhaps more so. But his mind no longer skittered; nowadays, it limped carefully from one anxiety to the next.

He wondered what the young man with the skittering mind would have made of the old man staring out from the back seat of his chauffeured car.

He wondered what happened at the end of that Maupassant story which had so struck him as a young man: the story about passionate, reckless love. Was the reader told the aftermath of the lovers' dramatic tryst? He must check, if he could find the book.

Did he still believe in Free Love? Perhaps so; theoretically; for the young, the adventurous, the carefree. But when children came along, you could not have both parents pursuing their own pleasure – not without causing unconscionable damage. He had known couples who were so set on their own sexual freedom that their children had ended up in orphanages.

That cost was far too high. So there had to be some accommodation. This was what life consisted of, once you got past the part where everything smelt of carnation oil. For instance, one partner might practise Free Love while the other looked after the children. More often it was the man who took such freedom; but in some cases it was the woman. That was how his own case might look to someone from a distance, not knowing all the details. Such a spectator would see Nina Vasilievna away a lot, for work or pleasure, or both at the same time. She was not fitted for domesticity, Nita, neither by temperament nor habit.

One person could truly believe in the rights of another person – in their right to Free Love. But yes, between the principle and its implementation often lay some anguish. And so he had buried himself in his music, which took his entire attention and therefore consoled him. Though when he was present in his music he was inevitably absent from his children. And sometimes, it was true, he had had his own flirtations. More than flirtations. He had tried to do his best, which was all a man could do.

Nina Vasilievna had been so full of joy and life, so outgoing, so comfortable in her own skin, that it was hardly surprising others loved her too. This was what he told himself; and it was true, and quite understandable, if, at times, painful. But he also knew that she loved him, and had protected him from many things he was unable or unwilling to deal with himself; also, that she was proud of him. All this was important. Because that person looking in from the outside, who did not understand, would understand even less what happened when she died. She was away in Armenia with A. at the time and suddenly fell ill. He had flown out with Galya, but Nita had died almost as soon as they arrived.

To state just the facts: he had returned to Moscow by train with Galya. Nina Vasilievna's body was flown back, escorted by A. At the funeral all was black and white and scarlet: earth, snow, and red roses provided by A. At the graveside he held A. close to him. And stayed near to him – or rather, kept A. near to him – for the next month or so. And thereafter, when he went to visit Nita, there were often red roses from A. strewn all over the grave. He found the sight of them comforting. Some people would not understand this.

He had once asked Nita if she was planning to leave him. She had laughed and replied, 'Not unless A. discovers a new particle and wins the Nobel Prize.' And he had laughed too, not being able to calculate the likelihood of either event. Some would not understand that he had laughed. Well, this was no surprise.

There was one thing he did resent. When all of them were staying on the Black Sea, usually at different sanatoriums, A. would arrive in his Buick to take Nita for a drive. Such drives were not a problem. And he always had his music – he had the knack of finding a piano, wherever he was. A. did not drive, so he had a chauffeur. No, the chauffeur was not the problem either. The problem was the Buick. A. had bought the Buick from a repatriated Armenian. And he had been allowed to do so. That was the problem. Prokofiev was allowed his Ford; A. was allowed his Buick; Slava Rostropovich had been allowed an Opel, another Opel, a Land Rover and then a Mercedes. He, Dmitri Dmitrievich Shostakovich, was not permitted to have a foreign car. Over the years, he could choose between a KIM-10-50 and a GAZ-MI and a Pobeda and a Moskvich and a Volga . . . So yes, he envied A. the Buick with its chrome and leather and fancy lights and fins, and the different noise it made, and the stir it created wherever it went. It was almost like a physical being, that Buick. And his wife Nina Vasilievna, with golden eyes, was in it. And for all his principles, that too was sometimes a problem.

He found the Maupassant story, the one about love without boundaries, love without thought for the morrow. What he had forgotten was that on the morrow, the young garrison commandant was severely reprimanded for the fake emergency, and his entire battalion punished by being transferred to the other end of France. And then Maupassant had allowed himself to speculate on his own narrative. Perhaps this was not, as the writer had first presumed, a heroic tale of love worthy of Homer and the Ancients, but instead some cheap, modern story out of Paul de Kock; and perhaps the commandant was even now boasting to a messful of fellow officers about his melodramatic gesture and its sexual reward. Such contamination of romance was all too likely in the modern world, Maupassant concluded; even if the initial gesture, and the night of love, remained, and had their own purity.

He pondered the story, and thought back over some of the things that had happened in his life. Nita's joy in another's admiration; her joke about the Nobel Prize. And now he wondered if perhaps he should see himself differently: as Monsieur Parisse, that businessman husband, locked out of the town, obliged at bayonet point to spend a night in the waiting room of Antibes railway station.

He switched his attention back to the chauffeur's ear. In the West, a chauffeur was a servant. In the Soviet Union, a chauffeur was a member of a well-paid and dignified profession. After the war, many chauffeurs were engineers with military experience. You knew to treat your chauffeur with respect. You never criticised his driving, or the state of the car, because the slightest such comment often resulted in the car being laid up for a fortnight with some mysterious illness. You also ignored the fact that when you did not require your chauffeur, he was probably off working on his own account, making extra money. So you deferred to him, and this was right: in certain respects, he was more important than you. There were chauffeurs so successful that they had their own chauffeurs. Were there composers so successful that they had others to compose for them? Probably; such rumours were common. It was said that Khrennikov was so busy being loved by Power that he only had time to sketch out his music, which others orchestrated for him. Perhaps this was the case, but if so, it did not matter very much: the music would be no better and no worse if Khrennikov had orchestrated it himself.

Khrennikov was still there. Zhdanov's stooge, who had so eagerly threatened and bullied; who had persecuted even his own former teacher Shebalin; who acted as if he personally signed every chit allowing composers to buy manuscript paper. Khrennikov, picked out by Stalin as one fisherman picks out another from afar.

Those obliged to play the customer to Khrennikov's shop clerk liked to tell a certain story about him. One day, the First Secretary of the Union of Composers was summoned to the Kremlin to discuss candidates for the Stalin Prize. The list had been drawn up as usual by the Union, but it was Stalin who made the final choice. On this occasion, and for whatever reason, Stalin decided not to play the avuncular Helmsman, but to remind the clerk of his own humble standing. Khrennikov was shown in; Stalin ignored him, pretending to work. Khrennikov became more and more anxious. Stalin looked up. Khrennikov mumbled something about the list of candidates. In return, Stalin 'gave him the eye', as they say. And immediately, Khrennikov shat himself. Panicked, and babbling some excuse, he fled from the presence of Power.

Outside, he found a couple of burly male nurses, well used to such a response, who grabbed him, took him to a special room, hosed him down, cleaned him up, let him recover himself, and gave him back his trousers.

Such behaviour was not, of course, abnormal. And you certainly did not despise a man for the weakness of his bowels when in the presence of a tyrant who could obliterate anybody on a whim. No, what you despised Tikhon Nikolayevich Khrennikov for was this: that he recounted his shame with rapture.

Now Stalin was gone, and Zhdanov was gone, and tyranny was repudiated – but Khrennikov was still there, unbudgeable, sucking up to the new bosses as he had sucked up to the old ones; admitting that, yes, some mistakes might have been made, but if so, all had happily been corrected. Khrennikov would outlast them all, of course, but some day even he would die. Unless this was one law of nature which didn't apply: perhaps Tikhon Khrennikov would live for ever, a permanent and necessary symbol of the man who loved Power and knew how to make it love him back. And if not Khrennikov himself, then his doubles and his descendants: they would live on for ever, regardless of how society changed.

He liked to think that he wasn't afraid of death. It was life he was afraid of, not death. He believed that people should think about death more often, and accustom themselves to the notion of it. Just letting it creep up on you unnoticed was not the best way to live. You should make yourself familiar with it. You should write about it: either in words or, in his case, music. It was his belief that if we thought about death earlier in our lives, we would make fewer mistakes.

Not that he hadn't made a lot of mistakes himself.

And sometimes he thought that he would have made the same number of mistakes even if he hadn't been so frequently concerned with death.

And sometimes he thought that death was indeed the thing that terrified him the most.

His second marriage: that had been one of his mistakes. Nita had died, and then, barely a year later, his mother had died. The two strongest female presences in his life: his guides, instructors, protectresses. He had been very lonely. His opera had just been murdered a second time. He knew that he was incapable of frivolous relationships with women; he needed a wife by his side. And so, while serving as chairman of the jury for Best Massed Choir at the World Festival of Youth, his eye had fallen on Margarita. Some said she resembled Nina Vasilievna, but he couldn't see it himself. She worked for the Communist Youth Organisation, and had perhaps been deliberately placed in his way, though that was no excuse. She had no knowledge of, and little interest in, music. She had tried to please, but failed. None of his friends liked her, or approved of the marriage, which of course had taken place suddenly and secretly. Galya and Maxim did not take to her – what could he expect, when she had so quickly replaced their mother? – and therefore she did not take to them. One day, when she was complaining about them, he said, with a completely straight face,

'Why don't we kill the children, then we can live happily ever after?'

She neither understood the remark, nor seemed to realise that it was humorous.

They separated, then divorced. It was not her fault: it was entirely his. He had put Margarita in an impossible position. In his loneliness, he had panicked. Well, that was nothing new.

As well as running volleyball competitions, he had also served as a tennis umpire. Once, at a sanatorium in the Crimea reserved for government officials, he had found himself in charge of a match involving General Serov, then head of the KGB. Whenever the general disputed a let or a line-call, he would take pleasure in his temporary authority. 'No arguing with the umpire,' he would command. This had been one of the few conversations with Power that he had enjoyed.

Had he been naive? Of course. But then, he had become so used to threats and intimidations and vile abuse that he was not as suspicious of praise and welcoming words as he should have been. Nor was he the only dupe. When Nikita the Corncob denounced the Cult of Personality, when Stalin's errors were acknowledged and some of his victims posthumously rehabilitated, when people started returning from the camps, and when *One Day in the Life of Ivan Denisovich* was published, how could men and women fail to hope? No matter that the toppling of Stalin meant the restoration of Lenin, that changes of political line were often merely intended to outflank rivals, and that Solzhenitsyn's novel was in his opinion reality varnished over, and the truth ten times worse: even so, how could men and women fail to hope, or believe that the new rulers were better than the old ones?

And that, of course, was the point at which the grabbing hands reached out towards him. See how things have changed, Dmitri Dmitrievich, how you are garlanded with honours, an ornament of the nation, how we let you travel abroad to receive prizes and degrees as an ambassador of the Soviet Union – see how we value you! We trust the dacha and the chauffeur are to your satisfaction, is there anything else you require, Dmitri Dmitrievich, have another glass of vodka, your car will be waiting however many times we clink glasses. Life under the First Secretary is so much better, would you not agree?

And by any scale of measurement, he had to agree. It *was* better, in the way that the life of a prisoner in solitary confinement is improved if he is given a cellmate, allowed to climb up to the bars and sniff the autumn air, and if the warder no longer spits in his soup – at least, not in the prisoner's presence. Yes, in that sense it was better. Which is why, Dmitri Dmitrievich, the Party wants to hug you to its bosom. We all remember how you were victimised during the Cult of Personality, but the Party has indulged in fruitful self-criticism. Happier times have come. So all we would like from you is an acknowledgement that the Party has changed. Which is not much to ask, is it, Dmitri Dmitrievich?

Dmitri Dmitrievich. All those years ago, he was intended to be Yaroslav Dmitrievich. Until his father and mother had allowed themselves to be talked out of the name by a bullying priest. You could say that his parents were merely displaying good manners, and proper piety, under their own roof. Or you could say that he had been born – or at least christened – beneath the star of cowardice.

★

The man they chose for his Third and Final Conversation with Power was Pyotr Nikolayevich Pospelov. Member of the Bureau of the Central Committee of the Russian Federation, chief ideologist of the Party throughout the Forties, former editor of *Pravda*, author of one of those books he had failed to read when tutored by Comrade Troshin. A plausible face with one of his six Orders of Lenin in his buttonhole. Pospelov had been a great supporter of Stalin until he became a great supporter of Khrushchev. He could explain fluently how Stalin's defeat of Trotsky had preserved the purity of Leninism in the Soviet Union. Nowadays Stalin was out of favour but Lenin was back in favour. A few more turns of the wheel and Nikita the Corncob would be out of favour; a few more after that and perhaps Stalin and Stalinism would be back. And the Pospelovs of this world – like the Khrennikovs – would sense each shift before it came, would have their ear to the ground and their eye to the main chance and their wetted finger in the air to apprehend any change of wind.

But that was no matter. What mattered was that Pospelov was his interlocutor in his final, and most ruinous Conversation with Power.

'I have excellent news,' Pospelov announced, drawing him to one side at some reception he had only attended because they had never stopped inviting him. 'Nikita Sergeyevich has personally announced an initiative to have you appointed Chairman of the Russian Federation Union of Composers.'

'That is far too great an honour,' he had instinctively replied.

'But not one, coming from the First Secretary, that you could possibly refuse.'

'I am not worthy of such an honour.'

'Perhaps it is not for you to judge your worthiness. Nikita Sergeyevich is better placed than you in this regard.'

'I could not possibly accept.'

'Come, come, Dmitri Dmitrievich, you have accepted high honours from across the world, which we have been gratified to see you accept. So I cannot possibly see how you can reject one offered by your own homeland.'

'I regret I have such little time. I am a composer, not a chairman.'

'It would take very little of your time. We would see to that.'

'I am a composer not a chairman.'

'You are our greatest living composer. Everyone acknowledges you as such. Your difficult years are behind you. That is why it is so important.'

'I do not follow you.'

'Dmitri Dmitrievich, we all know how you did not escape certain consequences during the Cult of Personality. Even though, if I may say so, you were more protected than most.'

'I can assure you that it didn't feel that way.'

'And this is why it is so important that you accept the chairmanship. To demonstrate that the Cult of Personality is over. To put it straightforwardly, Dmitri Dmitrievich, the changes wrought under the First Secretary, if they are to be made secure, need to be supported by public declarations and appointments such as the one proposed.'

'I am always happy to sign a letter.'

'You know that is not what I am asking.'

'I am unworthy,' he had repeated, adding, 'I am nothing but a worm beside the First Secretary.'

He doubted the allusion would be picked up by Pospelov, who indeed chuckled disbelievingly.

'I am sure we shall be able to overcome your natural modesty, Dmitri Dmitrievich. But we shall talk more at another time.'

Each morning, instead of prayer, he would recite to himself two poems by Evtushenko. One was 'Career', which described how lives are led beneath the shadow of Power:

> In Galileo's day, a fellow scientist
> Was no more stupid than Galileo.
> He was well aware that the Earth revolved,
> But he also had a large family to feed.

It was a poem about conscience and endurance:

> But time has a way of demonstrating
> The most stubborn are the most intelligent.

Was that true? He could never quite decide. The poem ended by marking the difference between ambition and artistic truthfulness:

> I shall therefore pursue my career
> By trying not to pursue one.

These verses both comforted and questioned him. He was, for all his anxieties and fearfulness and Leningrad civility, at base a stubborn man who had tried to pursue the truth in music as he had seen it.

But 'Career' was essentially about conscience; and his own accused him. What use, after all, is a conscience unless, like a tongue probing teeth for cavities, it seeks out areas of weakness, duplicity, cowardice, self-deception? If he went to the dentist every two months, always suspecting that something was wrong in his mouth, then he examined his conscience on a daily basis, always suspecting that something was wrong in his soul. There were many things to accuse himself of: acts of omission, fallings-short, compromises made, the coin paid to Caesar. At times he saw himself as both Galileo and that fellow scientist, the one with mouths to feed. He had been as courageous as his nature allowed; but conscience was always there to insist that more courage could have been shown.

He hoped, and tried, in the subsequent weeks, to avoid Pospelov, but there he was again one evening, coming towards him among the chat and the hypocrisy and the brimming glasses.

'So, Dmitri Dmitrievich, have you thought the matter over?'

'Oh, I am quite unworthy, as I told you.'

'I have passed on your agreement to seriously consider the chairmanship, and told Nikita Sergeyevich that only your modesty is holding you back.'

He paused to consider this distortion of their previous conversation, but Pospelov was hurrying on.

'Come, come, Dmitri Dmitrievich, there is a point at which modesty becomes a kind of vanity. We are counting on you to accept, and you will accept. Of course, as we both know, the chairmanship of the Russian Federation Union of Composers is not what this is about. And that is why I completely understand your hesitation. But we are all agreed that now the time has come.'

'What time has come?'

'Well, you cannot become chairman of the Union without joining the Party. It would be against all constitutional rules. Of course you knew that. It was why you hesitated. But I can assure you, there will be no obstacles put before you. It is really no more than a question of signing the application form. We shall take care of the rest.'

He felt, suddenly, as if all the breath had been taken out of his body. How, why had he not seen this coming? All through the years of terror, he had been able to say that at least he had never tried to make things easier for himself by becoming a Party member. And now, finally, after the great fear was over, they had come for his soul.

He tried to collect himself before replying, but even so, what he said came out in a rush.

'Pyotr Nikolayevich, I am quite unworthy, quite unsuitable. I do not have a political nature. I have to admit that I have never truly grasped the basic tenets of Marxism–Leninism. Indeed, they once appointed a tutor for me, Comrade Troshin, and I dutifully read all the books they provided, including, as I remember, one of yours, but I made such poor progress that I fear I must wait until I am better equipped.'

'Dmitri Dmitrievich, we all know about that unfortunate and – if I may say so – unnecessary appointment of a political tutor. So demeaning for you, and such a characteristic of life under the Cult of Personality. All the more reason to show how times have changed, and that members of the Party are not expected to have a deep grasp of political theory. Nowadays, under Nikita Sergeyevich, we all breathe more freely. The First Secretary is still a young man, and his plans extend over many years. It is important to us that you are seen to approve these new paths, this new freedom to breathe.'

He certainly felt little freedom to breathe at the moment, and reached for another defence.

'The truth is, Pyotr Nikolayevich, that I have certain religious beliefs which, as I understand it, are quite incompatible with Party membership.'

'Beliefs which you have wisely kept to yourself for many years, of course you have. And since they are not publicly known, this is not a problem we need to overcome. We shall not be sending you a tutor to help you with this . . . how shall I put it, this old-fashioned eccentricity.'

'Sergei Sergeyevich Prokofiev was a Christian Scientist,' he replied musingly. Aware that this was not strictly apropos, he then asked, 'You do not mean that you are going to reopen the churches?'

'No, I am not saying that, Dmitri Dmitrievich. But of course, now that sweeter air surrounds us, who knows what we shall soon be free to discuss. Free to discuss with our new and distinguished Party member.'

'And yet,' he replied, swerving from the numinous to the particular, 'and yet – you will correct me if I am wrong, but there is no overriding reason why a Union chairman has to be a Party member.'

'It would be inconceivable for this not to be the case.'

'And yet Konstantin Fedin and Leonid Sobolev are high up in the Union of Writers, and they are not Party members.'

'Indeed. But who has heard of Fedin and Sobelev compared to those who know the name of Shostakovich? This is not an argument. You are the most famous, the most celebrated of our composers. It would be inconceivable for you to be Union chairman without being a Party member. All the more so as Nikita Sergeyevich has such plans for the future development of music in the Soviet Union.'

Scenting a way out, he asked, 'What plans? I have read nothing about his plans for music.'

'Of course not. Because you will be invited to help the appropriate committee formulate them.'

'I cannot join a party which has banned my music.'

'What music of yours is banned, Dmitri Dmitrievich? Forgive me for not . . .'

'*Lady Macbeth of Mtsensk*. It was banned first under the Cult of Personality, and banned again after the Cult of Personality was overthrown.'

'Yes,' replied Pospelov soothingly, 'I can see how that might appear to be a difficulty. But let me speak to you as one practical man to another. The best way, the likeliest way, for you to get your opera performed is for you to join the Party. You have to give something to get something in this world.'

The man's slipperiness enraged him. And so he reached for his final argument.

'Then let me reply to you as one practical man to another. I have always said, and it has been one of the fundamental principles of my life, that I would never join a party which kills.'

Pospelov did not miss a beat. 'But that is precisely my point, Dmitri Dmitrievich. We – the Party – have changed. No one is being killed nowadays. Can you name me one person you know who has been killed under Nikita Sergeyevich? One single person? On the contrary, victims of the Cult of Personality are returning to normal life. The names of those who were purged are being rehabilitated. We need such work to continue. The forces of the camp of reaction are ever-present, and should not be underestimated. That is why we ask for your help – by joining the camp of progress.'

He left the encounter exhausted. Then, there was another

meeting. And another. It seemed that, wherever he turned, he saw Pospelov, glass in hand, coming towards him. The man even began to inhabit his dreams, always speaking in a calm, rational voice, and yet one driving him to madness. What had he ever wanted except to be left alone? He confided in Glikman, but not in his family. He drank, he was unable to work, his nerves were shredded. There was only so much a man could bear in his life.

1936; 1948; 1960. They had come for him every twelve years. And each of them, of course, a leap year.

'He could not live with himself.' It was just a phrase, but an exact one. Under the pressure of Power, the self cracks and splits. The public coward lives with the private hero. Or vice versa. Or, more usually, the public coward lives with the private coward. But that was too simple: the idea of a man split into two by a dividing axe. Better: a man crushed into a hundred pieces of rubble, vainly trying to remember how they – he – had once fitted together.

His friend Slava Rostropovich maintained that the greater the artistic talent, the better able it was to withstand persecution. Maybe that was true of others – certainly it was of Slava, who had in any case such an optimistic disposition. And who was younger, and did not know how it had been in earlier decades. Or what it was like to have your spirit, your nerve, broken. Once that nerve was gone, you couldn't replace it like a violin string. Something deep in your soul was missing, and all you had left was – what? – a certain tactical cunning, an ability to play the unworldly artist, and a determination to protect your music and your family at any price. Well, he finally thought – in a mood so drained of colour and resolution that it could scarcely be called a mood – perhaps this is today's price.

And so, he submitted to Pospelov, as a dying man submits to a priest. Or as a traitor, his mind numb with vodka, submits to a firing squad. He thought of suicide, of course, when he signed the paper put in front of him; but since he was already committing moral suicide, what would be the point of physical suicide? It wasn't even a question of lacking the courage to buy and hide and swallow the pills. It was rather that now, at this juncture, he lacked even the self-respect that suicide required.

But he was enough of a coward to run away, like the little boy slipping from his mother's grasp as they neared Jurgensen's hut. He signed the application form to join the Party, then fled to Leningrad and holed up with his sister. They could have his soul but not his body. They could announce that the distinguished composer had proved himself a true worm and joined the Party in order to help Nikita the Corncob develop his wonderful, if as yet perfectly unformed, ideas about the future of Soviet music. But they could announce his moral death without him. He would stay with his sister until it was all over.

Then the telegrams began to arrive. The official announcement would take place in Moscow on such-and-such a date. His presence was not just requested but required. No matter, he thought, I shall stay in Leningrad and if they want me in Moscow they will have to tie me up and drag me there. Let the world see how they recruit new Party members, by trussing them up and transporting them like sacks of onions.

Naive, as naive as any terrified rabbit. He sent a telegram saying he was unwell and regrettably unable to attend his own execution. They replied that the announcement would therefore wait until he was better. And in the meantime, of course, the news had slipped out and was all over Moscow. Friends telephoned, journalists telephoned: of which was he the more scared? And so, there is no escaping one's fate. And so, he returned to Moscow and read out yet another prepared statement, to the effect that he had applied to join the Party and that his petition had been granted. It seemed that Soviet power had finally decided to love him; and he had never felt a clammier embrace.

When he had married Nina Vasilievna, he had been too scared to tell his mother beforehand. When he had joined the Party, he had been too scared to tell his children beforehand. The line of cowardice in his life was the one thing that ran straight and true.

Maxim only ever saw his father weep twice: when Nina died, and when he joined the Party.

And so, he was a coward. And so, one spins around like a squirrel on a wheel. And so, he would put all his remaining courage into his music, and his cowardice into his life. No, that was all too . . . comforting. To say: Oh, excuse me, but you see I am a coward, there's really nothing I can do about it, Your Excellency, comrade, Great Leader, old friend, wife, daughter, son. That would make it uncomplicated, and life always refused simplicity. For instance, he had been afraid of Stalin's power, but not of Stalin himself: neither on the telephone, nor in person. For instance, he was capable of interceding for others where he would never dare intercede for himself. He surprised himself at times. So perhaps he was not entirely hopeless.

But it was not easy being a coward. Being a hero was much easier than being a coward. To be a hero, you only had to be brave for a moment – when you took out the gun, threw the bomb, pressed the detonator, did away with the tyrant, and with yourself as well. But to be a coward was to embark on a career that lasted a lifetime. You couldn't ever relax. You had to anticipate the next occasion when you would have to make excuses for yourself, dither, cringe, reacquaint yourself with the taste of rubber boots and the state of your own fallen, abject character. Being a coward required pertinacity, persistence, a refusal to change – which made it, in a way, a kind of courage. He smiled to himself and lit another cigarette. The pleasures of irony had not yet deserted him.

Dmitri Dmitrievich Shostakovich has joined the Communist Party of the Union of Soviet Socialist Republics. It can't be, because it couldn't ever be, as the major said when he saw the giraffe. But it could be, and it was.

He had always loved football, all through his life. He had long dreamt of composing an anthem for the game. He was a qualified referee. He kept a special notebook in which he recorded the season's results. In his younger days he had supported Dinamo, and once flew thousands of miles to Tbilisi just to watch a game. That was the point: you had to be there when it happened, surrounded by crowds of people all going mad and screaming. Nowadays, people watched football on television. To him, this was like drinking mineral water instead of Stolichnaya vodka, export strength.

Football was pure, that was why he had first loved it. A world constructed from honest striving and moments of beauty, with matters of right and wrong decided in an instant by a referee's whistle. It had always felt far away from Power and ideology and vacuous language and the despoiling of a man's soul. Except that – gradually, year by year – he became aware that this was just his fantasy, his sentimental idealisation of the game. Power made use of football just as it made use of everything else. So: if Soviet society was the best and most advanced in the history of the world, then Soviet football was expected to reflect this. And if it could not always be the very best, then it must at least be better than the football of those nations which had vilely abandoned the true path of Marxism–Leninism.

He remembered the 1952 Olympics in Helsinki, when the USSR had played Yugoslavia, fiefdom of the revisionist Gestapo thug Tito. To general surprise and dismay, the Yugoslavs had won 3–1. Everyone expected him to be downcast by the result, which he heard on the early morning radio in Komarova. Instead, he had rushed to Glikman's dacha and together they had demolished a bottle of finchampagne brandy.

But there had been more to the match than the result; it contained an example of the filth that pervaded everything under tyranny. Bashashkin and Bobrov: both in their late twenties, both stalwarts of the team. Anatoli Bashashkin, captain and centre half; Vsevolod Bobrov, the dashing scorer of five goals in the team's first three matches. In the defeat to

Yugoslavia, one of the opposition's goals had come as the result of a blunder by Bashashkin – that was true. And Bobrov had screamed at him, both on the pitch and afterwards,

'Tito's stooge!'

Everyone had applauded the remark, which might have been stupidly funny had not the consequences of denunciation been well known. And had Bobrov not been the best friend of Stalin's son Vasily. Tito's stooge versus Bobrov the great patriot. The charade had disgusted him. The decent Bashashkin was removed as captain, while Bobrov went on to become a national sporting hero.

The point was this: to some of those out there, to young composers and pianists, to optimists, idealists and the untarnished, what had Dmitri Dmitrievich Shostakovich looked like when he had applied to join the Party and was accepted? Khrushchev's stooge?

The chauffeur blew the horn at a car which seemed to be swerving towards them. The other car blew its horn back. There was nothing to be made from those two sounds, just a pair of mechanical noises. But out of most conjunctions and collaborations of sound he could make something. His Second Symphony had contained four blasts from a factory siren in F sharp.

He loved chiming clocks. He had a number of them, and liked to imagine a household in which all the clocks chimed together. Then, on the hour, there would be a golden blend of sound, a domestic, interior version of what it must have been like in old Russian towns and cities when all the church bells rang together. Assuming they ever did. Perhaps, this being Russia, half rang tardily, half in advance.

In his Moscow apartment, there were two clocks which struck at exactly the same moment. This was not chance. He would turn on the wireless a minute or two before the hour. Galya would be in the dining room, with the clock's door open, holding back the pendulum with one finger. He would be in his study, doing the same to the clock on his desk. When the time signal sounded, they each released their pendulum, and the clocks were united. He found such orderliness a regular pleasure.

He had once visited Cambridge, in England, as the guest of a former British ambassador to Moscow. The family also owned two chiming clocks, which announced their presence a minute or two apart. This had troubled him. He offered to adjust them, using the system he had devised with Galya, to make them synchronous. The ambassador had thanked him politely, but said that he rather preferred the clocks to strike separately: if you didn't quite hear the first one, you knew the other would be along soon enough to confirm whether it was three rather than four o'clock. Yes, of course he understood, but still it irked him. He wanted things to chime together. That was his fundamental nature.

He also loved candelabra. Chandeliers, fitted with real candles, not electric bulbs; and candlesticks bearing their single flickering flame. He enjoyed preparing them: making sure each candle stood at a true vertical, setting a match to the wicks in advance and then blowing them out, so they would be easier to relight when the big moment came. On his birthday there would be one flame for each year of his life. And friends knew the best present to bring. Khachaturian had once given him a splendid pair of branched candlesticks: bronze, with crystal pendants.

★

So, he was a man who loved chiming clocks and chandeliers. He had owned a private car since before the Great Patriotic War. He had a chauffeur and a dacha. He had lived with servants all his life. He was a member of the Communist Party and a Hero of Socialist Labour. He lived on the seventh floor of the Union of Composers building on Nezhdanova Street. Ever since he had been a Deputy of the Russian Federation, he had only to write a note to the manager of the local cinema for Maxim to be instantly granted two free tickets. He had access to the closed shops used by the nomen-klatura. He had been part of the organising committee for Stalin's seventieth birthday. Endorsements of the Party's policy on cultural matters often appeared over his name. He was shown in photographs hobnobbing with the political elite. He was still the most famous composer in Russia.

Those who knew him, knew him. Those who had ears could hear his music. But how did he seem to those who didn't know him, to the young who sought to understand the way the world worked? How could they not judge him? And how would he now appear to his younger self, standing by the road-side as a haunted face in an official car swept past? Perhaps this was one of the tragedies life plots for us: it is our destiny to become in old age what in youth we would have most despised.

He attended Party meetings as instructed. He let his mind wander during the endless speeches, merely applauding whenever others applauded. On one occasion, a friend asked why he had clapped a speech in the course of which Khrennikov had violently criticised him. The friend thought he was being ironic or, possibly, self-abasing. But the truth was, he hadn't been listening.

★

Those who did not know him, and who followed music only from a distance, might well have observed that Power had kept the deal offered by Pospelov on its behalf. Dmitri Dmitrievich Shostakovich had been received into the holy church of the Party, and little more than two years later, his opera – now retitled *Katerina Izmailova* – was approved and premiered in Moscow. *Pravda* piously commented that the work had been unfairly discredited during the Cult of Personality.

Other productions followed, at home and abroad. Each time, he imagined the operas he might have written had that part of his career not been killed. He might have set not just 'The Nose', but the whole of Gogol. Or at least 'The Portrait', which had long fascinated and haunted him. It was the tale of a talented young painter called Chartkov, who sells his soul to the devil in exchange for a bag of gold roubles: a Faustian pact which brings success and fashionability. His career is contrasted with that of a fellow art student who long ago disappeared to work and learn in Italy, and whose integrity is matched by his obscurity. He never returns, but one day sends home for exhibition a single work; it puts the whole of Chartkov's oeuvre to shame – and Chartkov knows it. The story's almost biblical moral is this: 'He who has talent in him must be purer in soul than anyone else.'

In 'The Portrait' there was a clear, two-way choice: integrity or corruption. Integrity is like virginity: once lost, never recoverable. But in the real world, especially the extreme version of it he had lived through, things were not like this. There was a third choice: integrity *and* corruption. You could be both Chartkov and his morally shaming alter ego. Just as you could be both Galileo and his fellow scientist.

★

In the time of Tsar Nicolas I a hussar had once abducted a general's daughter. Worse – or better – he had actually married her. The general had complained to the Tsar. Nicolas resolved the problem by decreeing first, that the marriage was null and void; secondly, that the girl's virginity was officially restored. Anything was possible in the homeland of elephants. But even so, he did not think there was a ruler, or a miracle, that could restore his virginity.

Tragedies in hindsight look like farces. That was what he had always said, always believed. And his own case was no different. He had, at times, felt that his life, like that of many others, like that of his country, was a tragedy; one whose protagonist could only solve his intolerable dilemma by killing himself. Except that he had not done so. No, he was not Shakespearean. And now that he had lived too long, he was even beginning to see his own life as a farce.

As for Shakespeare: he wondered, looking back, if he hadn't been unfair. He had judged the Englishman sentimental because his tyrants suffered guilt, bad dreams, remorse. Now that he had seen more of life, and been deafened by the noise of time, he thought it likely that Shakespeare had been right, had been truthful: but only for his own times. In the world's younger days, when magic and religion held sway, it was plausible that monsters might have consciences. Not any more. The world had moved on, become more scientific, more practical, less under the sway of the old superstitions. And tyrants had moved on as well. Perhaps conscience no longer had an evolutionary function, and so had been bred out. Penetrate beneath the modern tyrant's skin, go down layer after layer, and you will find that the texture does not change, that granite encloses yet more granite; and there is no cave of conscience to be found.

Two years after he joined the Party, he married again: Irina Antonovna. Her father had been a victim of the Cult of Personality; she herself was brought up in an orphanage for children of enemies of the state; now she worked in music publishing. There were some slight impediments: she was twenty-seven, only two years older than Galya, and already married to another older man. And of course this third marriage was as impulsive and secretive as his other two. But it was a novelty for him to have a wife who loved both music and domesticity, and who was as practical and efficient as she was adorable. He became shyly, tenderly uxorious.

They had promised to leave him alone. They never left him alone. Power continued speaking to him, but it was no longer a conversation, merely something one-sided and basely quotidian: a wheedling, a cajoling, a nagging. Nowadays, a late-night ring at the door meant not the NKVD or the KGB or the MVD, but a messenger scrupulously bringing him the text of an article he had written for the next morning's *Pravda*. An article he hadn't written, of course, but which required his signature. He would not even glance at it, merely scribble his initials. And the same went for the more scholarly articles which appeared under his name in *Sovetskaya Muzyka*.

'But what will this mean, Dmitri Dmitrievich, when they publish your collected writings?' 'It will mean that they are not worth reading.' 'But ordinary people will be misled.' 'Given the scale on which ordinary people have already been misled, I would say that a musicological article purportedly but not actually written by a composer does not matter much either way. In my view, if I were to read it and make a few corrections, that would be more compromising.'

But there was worse than this, much worse. He had signed a filthy public letter against Solzhenitsyn, even though he admired the novelist and reread him constantly. Then, a few years later, another filthy letter denouncing Sakharov. His signature appeared alongside those of Khachaturian, Kabalevsky and, naturally, Khrennikov. Part of him hoped that no one would believe – no one could believe – that he actually agreed with what the letters said. But people did. Friends and fellow musicians refused to shake his hand, turned their backs on him. There were limits to irony: you cannot sign letters while holding your nose or crossing your fingers behind your back, trusting that others will guess you do not mean it. And so he had betrayed Chekhov, and signed denunciations. He had betrayed himself, and he had betrayed the good opinion others still held of him. He had lived too long.

He had also learnt about the destruction of the human soul. Well, life is not a walk across a field, as the saying goes. A soul could be destroyed in one of three ways: by what others did to you; by what others made you do to yourself; and by what you voluntarily chose to do to yourself. Any single method was sufficient; though if all three were present, the outcome was irresistible.

★

He thought of his life as arranged into twelve-year cycles of bad luck. 1936, 1948, 1960 . . . Twelve more years led to 1972, inevitably another leap year, and so one in which he had confidently expected to die. He had certainly done his best. His health, always poor, declined to the point where he was unable to walk up stairs. He had been forbidden alcohol and cigarettes, prohibitions which in themselves were surely enough to kill a man. And vegetarian Power tried to help, ordering him from one end of the country to the other, to attend this premiere, receive that honour. He finished the year in hospital with kidney stones, while also enjoying radiotherapy for a cyst on the lung. He was stoic as an invalid; what troubled him was not so much his condition as people's reactions to it. Pity embarrassed him just as much as praise ever had.

However, he seemed to have misunderstood: the bad luck 1972 intended for him was not his dying, rather his continued living. He had done his best, but life had not yet finished with him. Life was the cat that dragged the parrot downstairs by its tail; his head banged against every step.

When these times are over . . . if they ever will be, at least until 200,000,000,000 years have passed. Karlo-Marlo and their successors were always denouncing the internal contradictions of capitalism, which would assuredly, logically, bring it crumbling down. And yet capitalism was still standing. Anyone with eyes to see would have been aware of the internal contradictions of Communism; but who knew if they would be enough to bring it down. All he could be sure of was that when – if – these times were over, people would want a simplified version of what had happened. Well, that was their right.

★

One to hear, one to remember, and one to drink – as the saying went. He doubted he could stop drinking, whatever the doctors advised; he could not stop hearing; and worst of all, he could not stop remembering. He so wished that the memory could be disengaged at will, like putting a car into neutral. That was what chauffeurs used to do, either at the top of a hill, or when they had reached maximum speed: they would coast to save petrol. But he could never do that with his memory. His brain was stubborn at giving house-room to his failings, his humiliations, his self-disgust, his bad decisions. He would like to remember only the things he chose: music, Tanya, Nina, his parents, true and reliable friends, Galya playing with the pig, Maxim imitating a Bulgarian policeman, a beautiful goal, laughter, joy, the love of his young wife. He did remember all those things, but they were often overlaid and intertwined with everything he wanted not to remember. And this impurity, this corruption of memory, tormented him.

In later years, his tics and mannerisms increased. He could be calm and sit quietly with Irina; but put him on a platform, at an official function, even among a gathering of those entirely sympathetic to him, and he could barely keep still. He would scratch his head, cup his chin, force his index and little fingers into the flesh of his cheek; twitch and fidget like a man waiting to be arrested and taken away. When listening to his own music, he would sometimes cover his mouth with his hands, as if to say: Do not trust what comes out of my mouth, trust only what goes into your ears. Or he would catch himself plucking at his torso with his fingertips: as if pinching himself to see if he was dreaming; or as if scratching sudden mosquito bites.

★

His father, after whom he had been obediently named, was often in his mind. That gentle, humorous man who woke each morning with a smile on his face: he had been 'an optimistic Shostakovich' if ever there was one. Dmitri Boleslavovich would always feature in his son's memory with a game in his hand and a song in his throat; peering through his pince-nez at a pack of cards or a wire puzzle; smoking his pipe; watching his children grow. A man who never lived long enough to disappoint others, or for life to disappoint him.

'The chrysanthemums in the garden have long since faded . . .' and then – how did it go on? – yes, 'But love still lingers in my ailing heart.' The son smiled, but not as the father used to. He had a different sort of ailing heart, and had already suffered two attacks. A third was on its way, because he could now recognise the warning sign: when drinking vodka brought him no pleasure.

His father had died the year before he met Tanya: that was right, wasn't it? Tatyana Glivenko, his first love, who told him she loved him because he was pure. They had kept in touch, and in later years she used to say that if only they had met a few weeks earlier at the sanatorium, the whole course of their lives would have been different. Their love would have been so firmly established by the time they came to part that nothing could have eradicated it. This had been their destiny, and they had missed it, been cheated out of it by the calendar's chance. Perhaps. He knew how people liked to melodramatise their early lives, and to obsess retrospectively about choices and decisions which at the time they had made unthinkingly. He also knew that Destiny was only the words *And so.*

Still, they had been one another's first loves, and he

continued to think of those weeks at Anapa as an idyll. Even if an idyll only becomes an idyll once it has ended. At the dacha in Zhukhova, a lift had been installed to take him from the hallway directly to his room. However, this being the Soviet Union, laws and regulations insisted that a lift, even one in a private residence, could only be worked by a properly qualified lift attendant. And what did Irina Antonovna, who cared for him so wonderfully well, do about this? She enrolled at the appropriate school and studied until she received her final certificate. Who would have thought that it would be his destiny to be married to a qualified lift operator?

He was not making a comparison between Tanya and Irina, between first and last; that was not the point. He was devoted to Irina. She made everything as bearable and enjoyable for him as she could. It was just that his possibilities of life were now much reduced. Whereas in the Caucasus his possibilities of life had been unbounded. But this was just what time did to you.

Before he joined up with Tanya at Anapa, there had been that performance of his First Symphony in the public gardens at Kharkov. It was, by any objective standards, a disaster. The strings sounded thin; the piano couldn't be heard; the timpani drowned everything; the principal bassoon was embarrassingly bad, and the conductor complacent; early on, the entire city's dog population had joined in, and the audience was beside itself with laughter. And yet it was pronounced a great success. The ignorant audience applauded long and loud; the complacent conductor took the praise; the orchestra kept up the illusion of competence; while the composer was required to mount the stage and bow his thanks many times to one and all. True, he was very annoyed; equally true, he was young enough to enjoy the irony.

'A Bulgarian policeman ties his bootlaces!' Maxim would announce to his father's friends. The boy had always loved pranks and jokes, catapults and air rifles; and over the years he had worked up this comic sketch to perfection. He would come on, his laces hanging loose, carrying a chair which he would frowningly arrange in the middle of the room, slowly moving it to the best position. Then, putting on a pompous face, and using both hands, he would lift and lever his right foot up on to the chair. He would look around, very pleased by this simple triumph. Then, with an awkward manoeuvre which the spectators might not at first understand, he would bend over, ignoring the foot on the chair, and tie the laces of the other shoe, the one flat on the floor. Immensely pleased with the result, he would swap legs, lifting his left foot up on to the chair before bending down to tie the laces of his right shoe. When he had finished, and the audience was squealing with pleasure, he would stand upright, almost to attention, scrutinise his two successfully laced boots, nod to himself, and ponderously carry the chair back to its place.

People found it so funny, he suspected, not just because Maxim was a natural comedian, not just because they enjoyed Bulgarian jokes, but for another, deeper reason: because the little sketch was so perfectly suggestive. Over-complicated manoeuvres to achieve the simplest of ends; stupidity; self-congratulation; imperviousness to outside opinion; repetition of the same mistakes. Did not all this, magnified across millions and millions of lives, mirror how things had been under the sun of Stalin's constitution: a vast catalogue of little farces adding up to an immense tragedy?

Or, to take a different image, one from his own childhood: that summer house of theirs at Irinovka, on that estate rich from the swathes of peat beneath it. The house from some dream or nightmare, with vast rooms and tiny windows, which made adults laugh and children shiver with fright. And now he realised that the country in which he had lived for so long was like that too. It was as if, when drawing up their plans for Soviet Russia, the architects had been thoughtful, meticulous and well-intentioned, but had failed at a very basic level: they had mistaken metres for centimetres, and sometimes the other way round. With the result that the House of Communism was built all disproportionate, and lacking in human scale. It gave you dreams, it gave you nightmares, and it made everyone – adults and children alike – fearful.

That phrase, so painstakingly applied by the bureaucrats and musicologists who had examined his Fifth Symphony, would be better attached to the Revolution itself, and the Russia that had come out of it: an optimistic tragedy.

Just as he could not control his mind's rememberings, he could not prevent its constant, vain interrogations. The last questions of a man's life do not come with any answers; that is their nature. They merely wail in the head, factory sirens in F sharp.

So: your talent lies beneath you like a swathe of peat. How much have you cut? How much remains uncut? Few artists cut only the best sections; or even, sometimes, recognise them as such. And in his own case, thirty years and more ago, they had erected a barbed-wire fence with a warning sign: DO NOT CROSS THIS POINT. Who knew what lay – what might have lain – beyond the wire?

A related question: how much bad music is a good composer allowed? Once, he thought he knew the answer; now, he had no idea. He had written a lot of bad music for a lot of very bad films. Though you could say that his music's badness made those films even worse, and thus rendered a service to truth and art. Or was that just sophistry?

The final wail in his head was about his life as well as his art. It was this: at what point does pessimism become desolation? His last chamber works articulated that question. He told the violist Fyodor Druzhinin that the first movement of his Fifteenth Quartet should be played 'so that flies drop dead in mid-air, and the audience start leaving the hall from sheer boredom'.

All his life he had relied on irony. He imagined that the trait had been born in the usual place: in the gap between how we imagine, or suppose, or hope life will turn out, and the way it actually does. So irony becomes a defence of the self and the soul; it lets you breathe on a day-to-day basis. You write in a letter that someone is 'a marvellous person' and the recipient knows to conclude the opposite. Irony allows you to parrot the jargon of Power, to read out meaningless speeches written in your name, to gravely lament the absence of Stalin's portrait in your study while behind a half-open door your wife is holding herself in against forbidden laughter. You welcome the appointment of a new Minister of Culture by commenting that there will be especial rejoicing in progressive musical circles, which have always placed their greatest hopes in him. You write a final movement to your Fifth Symphony which is the equivalent of painting a clown's grin on a corpse, then listen with a straight face to Power's response: 'Look, you can see he died happy, certain of the righteous and inevitable triumph of the Revolution.' And part of you believed that as long as you could rely on irony, you would be able to survive.

For instance, in the year in which he joined the Party, he wrote his Eighth Quartet. He told his friends that in his mind the work was dedicated 'to the memory of the composer'. Which would clearly have been regarded by the musical authorities as unacceptably egotistical and pessimistic. And so the dedication on the published score eventually read: 'To the Victims of Fascism and War'. This would no doubt have been viewed as a great improvement. But all he had really done was turn a singular into a plural.

However, he was no longer so sure. There could be a smugness to irony, as there could be a complacency to protest. A farm boy throws an apple core at a passing, chauffeur-driven car. A drunken beggar pulls down his trousers and bares his bottom to respectable folk. A distinguished Soviet composer inserts subtle mockery into a symphony or a string quartet. Was there a difference, either in motive, or in effect?

Irony, he had come to realise, was as vulnerable to the accidents of life and time as any other sense. You woke up one morning and no longer knew if your tongue was in your cheek; and even if it was, whether that mattered any more, whether anyone noticed. You imagined you were issuing a beam of ultraviolet light, but what if it failed to register because it was off the spectrum known to everyone else? He had inserted into his first cello concerto a reference to 'Suliko',

Stalin's favourite song. But Rostropovich had played straight over it without noticing. If the allusion had to be pointed out to Slava, who else in the world would ever spot it?

And irony had its limits. For instance, you could not be an ironic torturer; or an ironic victim of torture. Equally, you couldn't join the Party ironically. You could join the Party honestly, or you could join it cynically: those were the only two possibilities. And to an outsider, it might not matter which was the case, because both might seem contemptible. His younger self, by the side of the road, would see in the back of that car some wizened old sunflower, no longer turning towards the sun of Stalin's constitution, but still heliotropic, still drawn to the light-source of Power.

If you turned your back on irony, it curdled into sarcasm. And what good was it then? Sarcasm was irony which had lost its soul.

Beneath the glass of his desktop at the dacha in Zhukhova was an enormous photograph of Mussorgsky looking ursine and disapproving: it urged him to throw away inferior work. Beneath the glass of his desktop at his Moscow apartment was an enormous photograph of Stravinsky, the greatest composer of the century: it urged him to write the best music he could. And always, on his bedside table, was that postcard he had brought back from Dresden: of Titian's *The Tribute Money*.

The Pharisees had tried to trick Jesus by asking him if the Jews ought to pay taxes to Caesar. As Power, throughout history, always tried to dupe and subvert those it felt threatened by. He himself had tried not to fall for Power's tricks, but he was not Jesus Christ, only Dmitri Dmitrievich Shostakovich. And while Jesus's reply to the Pharisee who showed him Caesar's golden image was in fact usefully ambiguous – he did not specify what exactly belonged to God and what to Caesar – this was not a line he could repeat himself. 'Render unto art that which is art's?' Such was the creed of art for art's sake, of formalism, egocentric pessimism, revisionism, and all the other -isms thrown at him down the years. And Power's reply would always be the same: 'Repeat after me,' it would say, 'ART BELONGS TO THE PEOPLE – V. I. LENIN. ART BELONGS TO THE PEOPLE – V. I. LENIN.'

And so, he would die soon, probably during the next leap year. Then, one by one, they would all die: his friends and enemies; those who understood the complexities of life under tyranny, and those who would have preferred him to be a martyr; those who knew and loved his music, and a few old men who still whistled 'The Song of the Counterplan' without even knowing who had written it. All would die – except, perhaps, Khrennikov.

During his last years, he increasingly used the marking *morendo* in his string quartets: 'dying away', 'as if dying'. It was how he marked his own life too. Well, few lives ended fortissimo and in the major. And no one died at the right time. Mussorgsky, Pushkin, Lermontov – they had all died too soon. Tchaikovsky, Rossini, Gogol – they all should have died earlier; perhaps Beethoven as well. It was, of course, not just a problem for famous writers and composers, but for ordinary people too: the problem of living beyond your best span, beyond that point where life can no longer bring joy, instead only disappointment and dreadful happenings.

So, he had lived long enough to be dismayed by himself. This was often the way with artists: either they succumbed to vanity, thinking themselves greater than they were, or else to disappointment. Nowadays, he was often inclined to think of himself as a dull, mediocre composer. The self-doubt of the young is nothing compared to the self-doubt of the old. And this, perhaps, was their final triumph over him. Instead of killing him, they had allowed him to live, and by allowing him to live, they had killed him. This was the final, unanswerable irony to his life: that by allowing him to live, they had killed him.

And beyond death? He felt like raising a silent glass with the toast, 'Here's hoping it doesn't get any better than this!' If death would come as a relief from life, with its fur-lined humiliations, he did not expect things would become less complicated. Look what had happened to poor Prokofiev. Five years after his death, just as the memorial plaques were being installed across Moscow, his first wife was instructing lawyers to get the composer's second marriage annulled. And on what grounds! The grounds being that ever since his return to Russia in 1936, Sergei Sergeyevich had been impotent. Therefore his second marriage couldn't have been consummated; therefore she, the first wife, was his only legal wife, and his only legal heir. She was even demanding an affidavit from the doctor who had examined Sergei Sergeyevich two decades previously that his incapacity had been established as an irrefutable fact.

But this was what happened. They came and delved

between your sheets. Hey, Shosti, do your prefer blondes or brunettes? They looked for any weakness, any filth they could find. And they would always find something. The gossips and myth-mongers had their own version of formalism, as defined by Sergei Sergeyevich Prokofiev: anything we cannot understand on first hearing is probably immoral and disgusting – that was their attitude. And they would do with his life what they wished.

As for his music: he didn't suffer from the illusion that time would separate the good from the bad. He did not see why posterity should be able to calibrate quality better than those for whom the music was written. He was too disillusioned for that. Posterity would approve what it would approve. He knew all too well how composers' reputations rose and fell; how some were wrongly forgotten, and others mysteriously immortal. His modest wish for the future was that 'The Chrysanthemums in the Garden Have Long Since Faded' would continue to make men weep, however badly it was sung through some cracked amplifier in a cheap cafe; while, further along the road, an audience might be silently moved by one of his string quartets; and that, perhaps, one day not long ahead, both audiences might overlap and mingle.

He had instructed his family not to concern themselves with his 'immortality'. His music should be played on its merit, not because of some posthumous campaign. Among the many petitioners who besieged him nowadays was the widow of a well-known composer. 'My husband is dead and I have nobody' – such was her constant refrain. She was always telling him that he only had to 'lift the receiver' and instruct this or that person to play her late husband's music. He had done so many times, at first out of pity and politeness, later just to get rid of the woman. But it was never enough. 'My husband is dead and I have nobody.' And so he would lift the receiver yet again.

But one day the familiar words had provoked more than the familiar exasperation in him. So he had replied solemnly, 'Yes . . . yes . . . And Johann Sebastian Bach had twenty children and they *all* promoted his music.'

'Exactly,' agreed the widow. 'And that is why his music is still being played today!'

What he hoped was that death would liberate his music: liberate it from his life. Time would pass, and though musicologists would continue their debates, his work would begin to stand for itself. History, as well as biography, would fade: perhaps one day Fascism and Communism would be merely words in textbooks. And then, if it still had value – if there were still ears to hear – his music would be . . . just music. That was all a composer could hope for. Whom does music belong to, he had asked that trembling student, and though the reply was written in capital letters on a banner behind her interrogator's head, the girl could not answer. Not being able to answer was the correct answer. Because music, in the end, belonged to music. That was all you could say, or wish for.

The beggar would be long dead by now, and Dmitri Dmitrievich had almost immediately forgotten what he had said. But the one whose name is lost to history remembered. He was the one who made sense of it, who understood. They were in the middle of Russia, in the middle of a war, in the middle of all kinds of suffering within that war. There was a long station platform, on which the sun had just come up. There was a man, half a man really, wheeling himself along on a trolley, attached to it by a rope threaded through the top of his trousers. The two passengers had a bottle of vodka. They descended from the train. The beggar stopped singing his filthy song. Dmitri Dmitrievich held the bottle, he the glasses. Dmitri Dmitrievich poured vodka into each glass; as he did so, a wristlet of garlic slipped into view. He was no barman, and the level of vodka in each glass was slightly different. The beggar saw only what came out of the bottle; while he was thinking how Mitya was always anxious to help others, though temperamentally incapable of helping himself. But Dmitri Dmitrievich was listening, and hearing, as he always did. So when the three glasses with their different levels came together in a single chink, he had smiled, and put his head on one side so that the sunlight flashed briefly off his spectacles, and murmured,

'A triad.'

And that was what the one who remembered had remembered. War, fear, poverty, typhus and filth, yet in the middle of it, above it and beneath it and through it all, Dmitri Dmitrievich had heard a perfect triad. The war would end, no doubt – unless it never did. Fear would continue, and unwarranted death, and poverty and filth – perhaps they too would continue for ever, who could tell. And yet a triad put together by three not very clean vodka glasses and their contents was a sound that rang clear of the noise of time, and would outlive everyone and everything. And perhaps, finally, this was all that mattered.

Author's note

Shostakovich died on 9 August 1975, five months before the start of the next leap year.

Nicolas Nabokov, his tormentor at the New York Peace Congress, was indeed funded by the CIA. Stravinsky's aloofness from the congress was not just 'ethic and esthetic', as his telegram maintained, but also political. As his biographer Stephen Walsh puts it, 'Like all White Russians in postwar America, Stravinsky . . . was certainly not going to jeopardise his hard-won status as a loyal American by the slightest appearance of supporting a pro-Communist propaganda exercise.'

Tikhon Khrennikov did not, as in Shostakovich's (fictional) apprehension, prove immortal; but he did the next best thing, running the Union of Soviet Composers from its refounding in 1948 to its eventual collapse, along with the rest of the Soviet Union, in 1991. Forty-eight years on from 1948, he was still giving slickly bland interviews, claiming that Shostakovich was a cheerful man who had nothing to be frightened of. (The composer Vladimir Rubin commented: 'The wolf cannot speak of the fear of the sheep.') Khrennikov never disappeared from view, nor lost his love of Power: in 2003, he was decorated by Vladimir Putin. He finally died in 2007, at the age of ninety-four.

★

Shostakovich was a multiple narrator of his own life. Some stories come in many versions, worked up and 'improved' over the years. Others – for instance, what happened at the Big House in Leningrad – exist only in a single version, told many years after the composer's death, by a single source. More broadly, truth was a hard thing to find, let alone maintain, in Stalin's Russia. Even the names mutate uncertainly: so, Shostakovich's interrogator at the Big House is variously given as Zanchevsky, Zakrevsky and Zakovsky. All this is highly frustrating to any biographer, but most welcome to any novelist.

The Shostakovich bibliography is considerable, and musicologists will recognise my two main sources: Elizabeth Wilson's exemplary, multi-faceted *Shostakovich: A Life Remembered* (1994; revised edition 2006), and *Testimony: The Memoirs of Shostakovich* as related to Solomon Volkov (1979). When published, Volkov's book caused a commotion in both East and West, and the so-called 'Shostakovich Wars' rumbled on for decades. I have treated it as I would a private diary: as appearing to give the full truth, yet usually written at the same time of day, in the same prevailing mood, with the same prejudices and forgettings. Other useful sources include Isaak Glikman's *Story of a Friendship* (2001) and Michael Ardov's interviews with the composer's children, published as *Memories of Shostakovich* (2004).

Elizabeth Wilson is paramount among those who have helped me with this novel. She supplied me with material I would never otherwise have come across, corrected many misapprehensions, and read the typescript. But this is my book not hers; and if you haven't liked mine, then read hers.

J. B.
May 2015